the ashleys

melissa de la cruz

th e ashleys
jealous?

aladdin mix

NEW YORK   LONDON   TORONTO   SYDNEY

ALADDIN MIX

Simon & Schuster Children's Publishing Division

1230 Avenue of the Americas, New York, NY 10020

Text copyright © 2008 by Melissa de la Cruz

Designed by Karin Paprocki

The text of this book was set in MrsEavesRoman.

Manufactured in the United States of America

First Aladdin Paperbacks edition April 2008

2 4 6 8 10 9 7 5 3 1

Library of Congress Control Number 2007939557

ISBN-13: 978-1-4169-3407-3

ISBN-10: 1-4169-3407-3

For my LA alpha girls,

Katie Davis, Tina Hay, and Mary Clare Williams

And NYC alpha boy Tom Dolby who brought us together

I'm always honored to sit at your lunch table!!

Jealousy is all the fun you think they had.

—Erica Jong

We have the playaz and we have the playa haters

Please don't hate me because I'm beautiful, baby.

—Notorious B.I.G.

WELCOME TO THE SEVENTH GRADE SOCIAL EXPERIMENT. Otherwise known from now on as "The Rank." Don't ask us what smells—it's probably just the new menu at the ref!

But on to business! Did you ever wonder if popularity can be bottled like cheap celebrity perfume? Well, we did too. And we decided to find out what exactly makes an it girl "it." What makes a golden girl shine? And why do we call them the Beautiful People when they exhibit so much Bad Behavior?

Here at Miss Gamble's, the Ones to Watch are the triple threat known as the Ashleys. When one of them coughs, all of us catch colds.

So what does it take to follow in their Jimmy Choo–clad footsteps? Buttery blond highlights? A whisper-thin Michael Stars cashmere sweater? A plaid uniform skirt hiked just high enough to show off a killer Mystic tan? An adoring Gregory Hall boyfriend?

We need to know!

That's why every week we will rank each seventh-grade girl according to her sociopopularity index. The girls will be ranked according to the Fab Four S's: Style, Social Presence, Smarts, and Smile, with a maximum of ten points for each category.

And the Ashleys aren't the only ones we're keeping an eye on—everyone in the class is fair game!

So the next time you think you can get away with wearing last year's tunic tops, think again! Check your self-esteem in the Lost and Found and make sure your air kisses land on the right cheeks! We'll be watching . . . and ranking!

the FRONT RUNNERS

#1 ASHLEY SPENCER

Back from the dead and better than ever! Ashley Spencer is the girl everyone wants to be and the one to beat.

STYLE: 10

Like the best trendsetters, she's always one haute-preppie step ahead of the game. Without her, we'd still be running around wearing thick socks and carrying mock Birkins.

SOCIAL PRESENCE: 10

Even near-death, she had poise. Extra cred for looking supercute even while almost meeting her maker.

SMILE: 10

The most dazzling smile this side of the Golden Gate Bridge, if we can be so cheesy.

SMARTS: 9

Not telling anyone about your life-threatening allergy? Seems just a *little* dumb.

CUMULATIVE SCORE: 39   (Hey, no one is perfect!)

#2 ASHLEY "A.A." ALIOTO

Gorgeous on the playing field as well as the dance floor, A.A. is the pinup with a heart of gold!

STYLE: 10

The girl with legs longer than a racehorse's is a tomboy bombshell, a perfect role "model."

SOCIAL PRESENCE: 8

We hear her online love fizzed out and she was left holding the iPhone. Aw!

SMILE: 10

Gets our vote for her killer looks and effervescent personality.

SMARTS: 9

Marilyn Monroe once said a smart girl is one who plays dumb!

CUMULATIVE SCORE: 37

next >>

#3 ASHLEY "LILI" LI

Watch out, world, this is the busiest seventh grader on the planet!

STYLE: 9

She's got it all: looks, charm, and an allowance larger than your parents' bank account.

SOCIAL PRESENCE: 8

Sometimes next to her two best friends, it's hard to see her light. Our advice? Come out and let it shine!

SMILE: 7

Hasn't done a lot of this lately, so we have to take points off for the furrow that's starting to appear between her brows.

SMARTS: 10

The Great One also has a Great Brain.

CUMULATIVE SCORE: 34

Well, it is called AshleyRank, isn't it?

But there are a few girls nipping at their heels. . . .

Here are some of our favorite dark horse candidates:

#7 SHERIDAN RILEY

She's been hero-worshipping the Ashleys for so long she could be mistaken for one of them. Not! Still, points for trying.

STYLE: 6

The helmet hairdo doesn't help, and often dresses as if Burberry threw up on her.

SOCIAL PRESENCE: 10

Knows everything about everyone and isn't afraid to dish.

SMILE: 7

Now that the braces are off, she's in fighting form.

SMARTS: 9

Nothing gets past this one.

CUMULATIVE SCORE: 32

next >>

#18 LAUREN PAGE

Last year we didn't even know her name, but things change fast. This girl proves there's hope for us all.

STYLE: 8

We're digging the new look and the new attitude.

SOCIAL PRESENCE: 7

Arrived at the fall mixer on the arm of Billy ("Oil Heir") Reddy and is rumored to be starring on her own reality TV show. But Billy isn't her BF, so does that mean her hot show is just a lot of hot air?

SMILE: 5

Has lots to smile about, but rarely does.

SMARTS: 9

Book-smart, sure, but does she have the wits to match?

CUMULATIVE SCORE: 29

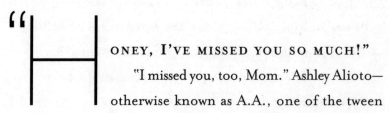

A MODEL HOMECOMING

"**H**ONEY, I'VE MISSED YOU SO MUCH!**"**

"I missed you, too, Mom." Ashley Alioto—otherwise known as A.A., one of the tween triumvirate of Ashleys who were the acknowledged social elite of Miss Gamble's School for Girls—smiled up at her mother.

Jeanine Alioto was as beautiful as ever, tall and willowy, her long dark hair perfectly razor-cut and blow-dried, her eyebrows immaculately threaded, her lips injected with just enough Venezuelan bee serum to make her mouth a seductive pout. Sometimes girls at school—non-Ashleys, of course—asked her if it was a drag having a former supermodel for a mother, as though getting great genes (not to mention an endless supply of great jeans) was a bad thing.

The only kind-of-bad part was when her mother disappeared for weeks at a time because some rich guy wanted her to sail around the Caribbean with him or hang out at the Cannes Film Festival. A.A. was left at home in their penthouse apartment in the Fairmont Hotel with her stepbrother, Ned. They got along just fine without Jeanine—duh, room service!— but it was always better when her mother was home, not least because she always brought back a ton of cool gifts.

"And these are for you, Lili," said her mother, pulling a chic pair of black shoes from one of her overflowing Goyard suitcases and tossing them into the eager hands of Ashley Li.

The shoes meant for Lili had three-inch curvy heels with ankle straps fastened by a tiny ribbon. Receiving designer swag was just another one of the many perks of being an Ashley, but Lili, perched on the edge of the butter-colored chaise lounge, peered at them with a puzzled smile on her face.

"Thanks so much, Jeanine," she said in her peppiest voice, but A.A. knew what she was thinking. Lili was a total brand queen, and if she didn't recognize the name imprinted in the soft calfskin soles of the shoes, then they might as well be a pair of sweaty Crocs. "Are these an Argentinian . . . er, specialty?"

"Sweetie, they're tango shoes!" Jeanine scrambled to her feet. In her calf-high Fiorentini & Baker boots tucked into skintight Ksubi jeans, she was more than six feet tall, tower-ing over the petite Lili and even over A.A., who'd inherited her mother's long, lean physique and was currently sprawled out on the white sheepskin rug. "I got them for A.A. and then remembered she'd rather throw herself around on a soccer field than do anything ladylike, and I know you're the same size. I spent a few days in Buenos Aires at the tango festival, and these are from *the* tango shoe store. Everything's handmade and super expensive."

"I'd love to learn the tango," said Lili with a sigh, flicking her glossy jet-black hair, a dreamy expression floating over her pretty, heart-shaped face. A.A. let out a snort of laughter—all Lili needed was yet another extracurricular activity! When she wasn't taking violin or tennis lessons, she was brushing up on her French and Mandarin language skills, or learning how to take expert photographs, or helping a Stanford professor with his genetics research. If A.A. had Lili's overscheduled life, she'd go crazy.

"I thought you were going to Brazil." A.A. picked at the intricately woven blue hammock her mother had pulled from suitcase number one twenty minutes ago. There was an outdoor terrace off the suite where it would hang perfectly.

"Rio in the off-season just isn't me." Jeanine sighed, mussing her luxuriant dark locks. "The Copa is no fun in the rain, and I was sick of looking at all those undernourished girls from Ipanema hanging around and hoping to get discovered by Victoria's Secret."

A.A. rolled onto her stomach and rested her head in her

hands. She loved it when her mother started dishing on the modeling world. Jeanine always called herself the Last of the Supermodels, talking about the good old days when the top models were known by their first names alone, everyone had major attitude and the breasts to go with it, and affairs with celebrities were de rigueur—her first husband, Ned's father, was a British rock star. These days, she said, the girls were barely old enough to date, and all the magazine covers were hogged by skanky Hollywood startlets.

"And anyway," Jeanine continued, back on her knees and rifling through her suitcase again, "Gil was thinking of buying some gaucho ranch in Argentina, so we flew down there."

Gil was Richard Gilbert, the software tycoon Jeanine had been dating on and off for the last six months. She and Ned had already decided they didn't want him as a stepfather, but it was too soon to worry—Jeanine's relationships had a habit of self-combusting before too many commitments were made.

"Did you and Mr. Gilbert learn to dance the tango while you were there?" Lili had already slipped off her Tory Burch flats and was carefully tying the delicate ribbons of the tango shoes around her slim ankles.

"I don't know what *Mr. Gilbert* was doing," said Jeanine, her voice dripping with sarcasm. "After three days galloping around in the mud wearing a poncho, I'd had enough. And let's just say horses weren't the only thing he was checking out in Argentina."

She tugged a vibrant purple-patterned silk scarf out of her bag and draped it over A.A.'s shoulders, and then rummaged for another one, this time a swirling, kaleidoscopic mix of greens and pinks.

"For you," Jeanine said, wafting it at Lili. "These are just Pucci—I picked them up at the airport when my flight back was delayed. I grabbed a blue one for Ashley, too, because I know how you three *have* to have the same things."

"So you and Gil have broken up?" A.A. tried not to sound too pleased. She sat up to adjust her trademark pigtails and loop the scarf around her neck.

"Let's just say I need someone who's man enough to tango with me and me alone," Jeanine said, rocking back on her heels and shooting them her famous wicked *Cosmo*-cover smile. "And you know what I always tell you, girls."

"Leave them while you're still looking good!" chorused A.A. and Lili, laughing. For the millionth time in her twelve years, A.A. felt relieved and happy that her mother was so much fun, more of a friend than a mom. It was so easy to talk to her. Everything was better when Jeanine was home—even if she did insist on redecorating their luxurious penthouse suite way too often. But as long as she didn't let her snooty decorator banish A.A. and Ned's vast video game collection or try to downsize the flat-screen TV in the loft-sized living room, they wouldn't complain.

"So what's been going on at Hogwarts?" her mother asked, pulling the Pucci scarf away from A.A. and tying it in an effortlessly chic headband around her own hair.

"Social Club had its first coed mixer with the Gregory Hall boys," Lili told her, "which I pretty much organized—"

"Pretty much nearly murdering Ashley at the same time," interrupted A.A., and then they both scrambled to fill Jeanine in on the crazy events of just a week ago. The vanilla cupcakes Lili ordered had triggered Ashley Spencer's serious nut allergy, and she'd ended up unconscious on the dance floor.

No one had known about Ashley's allergy, except A.A., who'd only remembered Ashley's secret when Ashley wannabe and terminal dork Lauren Page had asked if Ashley happened to be allergic to anything. If it hadn't been for quick thinking on Lauren's part, Lili would be facing a future in juvenile hall rather than Groton.

"Sounds like you all owe this girl Lauren," said Jeanine. Outside, a light rain pattered against the tiles of the terrace, and she reached for the remote control, instantly conjuring up a flickering fire in the white granite fireplace.

A.A. and Lili exchanged glances: That climber Lauren was still in social Siberia—that is, unless the Ashleys decided otherwise. Lili and A.A. were neutral on the subject, and Ashley had had other things on her mind since the dance.

Namely *one* other thing. Namely Tri Fitzpatrick. The boy that A.A. had known forever, her video-game buddy. The boy who was the cutest (and shortest) seventh grader at Gregory Hall. The boy who was supposed to be crushing on *her*, not on Ashley. Not that she was interested in him, so why did it bother her so much that he'd finally found someone who returned his affections?

"Anyway, Lauren's old news. Everyone's talking about something else now," A.A. told her mother. "At the beginning of this week, the weirdest thing happened."

"There's this new blog," Lili chimed in, her voice as animated as her face. "Nobody knows who's behind it!"

"But it's someone at our school, that much is obvious." A.A. pulled off her cashmere socks and wriggled her bare toes.

"It's like Facebook," Lili added breathlessly. "You have to check it every day, or every hour, or every five minutes!"

"Everyone's saying we're the ones who did it, but it's not true," A.A. said, looking at Lili, who shook her head vehemently.

"What are you girls talking about?" Jeanine asked, emptying her giant makeup bag onto the polished wood floor and grabbing a Chanel nail polish bottle before it rolled away.

"It's called AshleyRank," A.A. explained. "That's why everyone thinks the Ashleys started it."

"All the seventh-grade girls are ranked according to how cute and popular they are. Totally addictive. You know," Lili smirked, "like watching *Shark Week*. A feeding frenzy. Who gets to rule the ocean—or in this case, seventh grade." She reached into her beige Fendi Spy bag and retrieved her Blackberry, frowning a little as she tapped on the miniature screen. "Here it is. AshleyRank, one through thirty-six.

"Cass Franklin is number thirty-six," Lili said, her voice full of pity and condescension. She didn't have to check the blog again because she'd already memorized the key details.

"That's the girl I told you about," A.A. said to her mom. "The one who should be living in a plastic bubble. She has to keep an oxygen tank in her bag in case of emergency."

Jeannine looked concerned. "How awful!"

"Yeah. It's social death," Lili added.

A.A. laughed, then felt a little bad about laughing.

"More to the point," continued Lili, who looked a bit impatient, "the Ashleys hold the top three spots. That's why everyone thinks we came up with this."

"And you're sure you didn't?" Jeanine sounded amused.

"I know *I* didn't," said A.A.

"I certainly didn't." Lili was indignant, and A.A. knew why: Lili was the number three Ashley, behind A.A. and, at number one, the universally acknowledged Queen Bee of Miss Gamble's herself, Ashley Spencer.

The intercom chimed, and the front desk clerk announced another guest. A.A. told him to let her in: It was Ashley, arriving for her share of the South American fashion loot. The girl must have ESP. Jeanine was about to open the next suitcase and start pulling out fabulous clothes for her daughter to try on. Anything A.A. didn't want, Lili and Ashley could grab, and it was always funny watching them fight over A.A.'s leftovers.

The private elevator that opened directly into the apartment dinged.

"Hey, Ash, right on time as usual," A.A. called, looking up with a grin that soon disappeared from her pretty face.

Because when the elevator doors opened, and Ashley—cool, blond, and stylishly dressed, as usual—strolled in, she wasn't alone. Holding her hand in the most lame and embarrassing way, and gazing up at her with adoring puppy-dog eyes, as though they were actually, yuckily, *in love*, was Tri Fitzpatrick.

ALL'S FAIR IN LOVE
AND FASHION

T WAS *SO* TYPICAL OF ASHLEY TO BE LATE, thought Lili as A.A.'s very cool mom removed a conch-shell bikini from her luggage and tossed it to her daughter.

Lili laughed when A.A. blushed as she held the minuscule triangle top against her bountiful chest, but her mind was on her AshleyRank ranking.

She was so not happy about *that* at all. Lili hated to think she was lesser than anybody. She worked hard to get all As and keep her place in as many advanced classes as possible; plus, she was the head of the Honor Board at Miss Gamble's. Okay, so maybe in the small pond of the seventh-grade social circle she had to kowtow to Ashley Spencer. But with the emergence of this mysterious blog that had appeared out of nowhere, she was suddenly relegated to the bronze-medal position. She'd always thought she'd outranked A.A. *at least.*

It didn't matter that there were thirty-three names below hers, or that the talk at school was about how the Ashleys had nabbed all the top spots. Lili knew she could never be happy until her name was the one on the very tippy-top of the social pyramid.

Why did Ashley have to be number one on AshleyRank? If anyone else had fallen over at the dance, they would have been humiliated. And Lauren No-Friends Page had to get all *Grey's Anatomy* and stab Ashley with an EpiPen, bringing her back to life. (Not that Lili was sad that Ashley was alive, of course—which wasn't the same thing as being happy that Ashley might be dead.) But Ashley had managed to turn it into a social triumph, nabbing the hottest seventh grader at Gregory Hall. Why did she have to be the first of the Ashleys to have a real boyfriend? It just wasn't fair!

Lili sighed. She looked across the room, where Ashley and Tri were sitting on the other long sofa, leaning against each other. They looked pretty cute together, she had to admit. She'd always assumed Tri had a thing for A.A. since the two of them hung out so much, but maybe she was wrong after all. He looked better paired up with Ashley, anyway. Somehow, next to Ashley, he didn't seem quite so short. His hair was dark and hers was golden blond, and they were both gorgeous.

Tri was still wearing his Gregory Hall uniform—a white shirt and gray flannel pants, his blue and gold tie loosely knotted—but Ashley had gone home after school to change, of course. She was wearing her new Stitch jeans, a lace-trimmed cami, and a cute deep-V plaid hoodie from Limited Too. Earlier that day at school she'd told Lili that boys didn't like it if their girlfriends were dressed up all the time, like she was a total expert on boys all of a sudden!

"Tri, you're going to be very bored," A.A.'s mom was warning him. "We have a lot of clothes to get through here!"

"He doesn't mind," said Ashley in her bossiest voice, and Lili glanced over at Tri, wondering how he'd react to Ashley— sorry, his *girlfriend*—speaking for him. But he didn't seem to mind.

"I'll just suffer in silence, Mrs. A," he said, not taking his eyes off Ashley. A.A. was glaring at him from across the expansive coffee table. Lili noticed that whenever Ashley and Tri were together, A.A. always found some way to excuse herself. But there was no escape this time.

Lili wished Ashley hadn't brought Tri either. She didn't want a guy there while they were trying on clothes. How exactly were they going to do this with a boy in the room?

"I know what we'll do," said A.A.'s mom, reading Lili's

18

mind. "A.A., why don't you drag over that shoji screen, and you girls can get changed behind it so Tri doesn't have to keep closing his eyes."

"That's a great idea," said Lili, knowing that she couldn't have gotten dressed and undressed in front of a boy. She didn't even have any brothers—she was the middle child in a family of five daughters, with a father who spent most of his time in his huge, book-lined study when he wasn't spending long hours at work.

"I'll help you," offered Tri, but A.A. shrugged her shoulders and gave a dismissive snort.

"Thanks but no thanks." A.A. was practically scowling. "I don't need *your* help." Lili saw A.A.'s face flush red, even though she wasn't sitting anywhere near the fireplace.

A.A. strode across the room to the Japanese folding screen. It was made from gold silk, and three elegant flying cranes were etched into the fine fabric. Two years ago Jeanine had filmed a cell phone commercial in the country and had it shipped back as part of her shopping bounty; she'd said the screen was an antique, from a geisha house in Kyoto.

The screen was taller than A.A., and she was struggling to close and lift it, but she was clearly determined to manage without Tri's help.

"C'mon, let me get it," Tri said, getting up from the couch and picking up the other end of the screen.

"Oh, all right!" A.A. huffed, looking put out.

"What's with you?" Tri asked, an annoyed edge to his voice.

"Nothing!" said A.A., puffing her cheeks as they pushed the screen across the room.

"Are you sure?" he insisted, looking straight at A.A. as if seeing her for the first time that afternoon. That dreamy glaze—the one that had been on his face since the night of the dance, almost as if he'd been hypnotized by Ashley—was gone for a moment.

"Positive. I just—I wish you hadn't—," A.A began to say.

"What?"

"Nothing!"

Tri looked frustrated as he picked up his edge of the screen.

Lili thought maybe A.A. had changed her mind about Tri. A.A. had always sworn she didn't like him "that way," but maybe she was finally seeing him in a different light. Could she even be jealous of Ashley? A.A. had certainly been cheerful all day until the elevator doors opened and Ashley had flounced in with Tri on her arm.

"Is over here good?" Tri asked after dragging the screen across the rug and setting it down by the glass doors to the terrace. His forehead looked a little sweaty, since he'd done most of the lifting.

A.A. grunted as if she couldn't care less, not even trying to hide her irritation as she plopped down on a low, squishy stool near Lil rather than returning to the sofa.

"I don't care about stripping down myself," Jeanine told them, holding up a silk blouse and scrutinizing it. "Backstage at a fashion show, you're naked eighty percent of the time. You can't even wear undies in case they show through a dress."

"Mom!" said A.A., looking sharply at Tri.

"TMI," Tri joked, giving Ashley a squeeze.

"Maybe Tri should leave—this is a girl thing," A.A. mumbled, but only Lili heard her—Ashley was squealing and trying to pry Tri's hands away, while Jeanine was laughing because she'd embarrassed him.

And then it was time to try on clothes. A.A. took up her post behind the screen, and Jeanine hurled outfit after outfit over to her. Whatever A.A. didn't want, she threw back into the room.

Ashley soon forgot about cuddling up with Tri, Lili noticed; she abandoned him and moved into receiver position near the screen, trying to edge Lili out. As soon as they'd grabbed a couple of items, they headed behind the screen to join A.A., pulling on tops and skirts, wriggling into perfect little dresses, knocking elbows and hips as they struggled to change clothes.

"Maybe I should be the one behind the screen," Tri called. Nobody responded; this was no time for jokes.

Every time Ashley pulled on a different outfit, she'd sashay out to pose for Tri. "What do you think?" she asked, coming out in a red flamenco dress.

"You look great," he told her. He said that about everything she put on, almost automatically.

Hidden behind the screen, A.A. stuck her finger in her mouth and mimed gagging.

Lili sniggered, but A.A. didn't laugh. She was really in a funk now, barely bothering to try on most of the clothes. Lili wished she would lighten up already. This was supposed to be fun.

"I'm tired," A.A. said, taking off the ruffled silk camisole she was wearing and throwing it to the ground. She put on her stretchy T-shirt again and walked out from behind the screen. "I'm done, Mom. Whatever else you have in the bag can go to Ashley or Lili."

Lili followed, stopping to retrieve the cami. She sat on the edge of the chaise, deciding to try on her tango shoes again to see how they'd look with the Phillip Lim minidress she'd managed to tug out of Ashley's greedy hands. Ashley was spinning around by the sofa, modeling the twirly Temperley skirt A.A. had rejected as too girly.

"All right, last items, ladies," said Jeanine, rocking back

on her heels. "It's Chloé, but I guess I don't need to tell you two that."

Lili stopped fiddling with the ribbons on her shoes. In Jeanine's hands was the most perfect weathered, shrunken leather jacket in a creamy caramel color. Three-quarter sleeves, old-school wool collar, with hidden zippers and a fitted waist. From underneath it peeped a poufy bubble dress with mirrored detailing. It was amazing. Lili *had* to have it.

"I'll try it—," she began, scrambling to her feet, but Ashley had leaped through the air somehow and was bearing down on the jacket. As Lili grabbed the left shoulder, Ashley took possession of the right sleeve.

"Why don't you both try it on?" Jeanine suggested, and to Lili's surprise, Ashley stepped back.

"You first, Lil," she said, smiling like a crocodile. Lili slipped behind the Japanese screen and took off her Luella button-down and Da-Nang capris. She slipped on the dress, which floated on her body, and zipped up the jacket. It fit her beautifully, though the sleeves were maybe a little long—Jeanine had bought it with long-limbed A.A. in mind. The skirt hit right at the knees, the fabric draping against her legs. She stepped into the room and did a slow twirl for her audience.

"Is it almost over?" groaned Tri, slumping lower in his seat.

"No one's making you stay," A.A. snapped at him.

23

Ashley, still beaming, walked over and stroked one of the jacket's soft sleeves.

"Yummy!" she gushed, and then clicked her fingers. "My turn."

Five minutes later Ashley emerged from the makeshift dressing room, her eyes sparkling in triumph.

"I hate to say this," she said with a toss of her long blond hair, "because I know it sounds so conceited. But you have to admit, Lil—this looks way better on me."

Lili opened her mouth to protest, but no words came out. Because Ashley was right. It did look better on her. The proportions of the jacket suited her more, and the skirt was an inch shorter, the perfect length.

"It'll look perfect with my new crocodile boots," she told Jeanine. "Don't you think it suits me best?"

A.A.'s mother shook her head and laughed.

"You girls have to sort it out," she said. "This is more tiring than a twelve-hour flight. A.A., darling, will you call down for some herbal tea?"

"So what do you say, Lil?" Ashley asked.

"I guess," said Lili uncertainly, flopping down on the lounge chair, defeated. And that was it—decided just like that. What Ashley wanted, Ashley got. Clothes, bags, jewelry, boyfriends. Lili just didn't know how much longer she could stand it.

ASHLEY'S NOT THE KIND OF GIRL WHO HUGS IT OUT

ASHLEY SPENCER SMILED AS SHE folded up all of her loot. She had the best possible life.

She had parents who doted on her, a beautiful, art-filled house that overlooked San Francisco Bay, house staff that had known her all her life and did everything for her, every item of clothing and every gadget she wanted—even if she only wanted it for five minutes. To top it all off, she was Ashley Spencer, the most important Ashley in the most envied clique in the most exclusive school in San Francisco. And now she was the first of the Ashleys to snag a real boyfriend, and an incredibly cute one at that. Plus, he adored her completely.

And why wouldn't he? It was no wonder she was top

dog—excuse her, top biatch—on AshleyRank. Could life be more perfect?

Okay—so some things could be better. She could have a cool model mom like A.A.'s, who spent most of the time flying off to glam locations and came home only long enough to empty The. Best. Clothes. Ever. from her suitcases. And today Ashley totally scored the best of the best! She'd known that Lili would back down. She always did. Everything was the way it should be: She could hang with her girls and—even better—she could hang with her guy.

Her guy! Who knew Tri was *so* funny? She looked at him affectionately as she patted a particularly choice Pringle sweater that she'd scored because it made A.A. look too chesty.

Tri had made the funniest comments about the outfits she was trying on all afternoon. When she came out in leggings and a swing dress, he asked her if she meant to look like a lampshade. He had no idea at all about the ruched arm warmers—"My wrists never get cold," he said, screwing up his adorable face—and the detachable collar on the Burberry ribbed sweater jacket confounded him completely, poor boy. "Is it a shirt or a sweater?" he asked, amused. "How do you guys know what to do with all this stuff?"

"Isn't he so cute?" Ashley had asked A.A. as she ruffled Tri's hair. Sure, he was short, but guys who were short in junior high were like girls with flat chests—they were going to grow. Her Dad told her once that he was the shortest guy in his class all the way through ninth grade, and now he was over six feet tall. Ashley hoped that Tri wouldn't be a mini-hottie for quite that long, but she could cope with him staying Elijah Wood–size for the foreseeable future.

A.A. had only snorted. What was wrong with her? A.A. wasn't really into all the clotheshorse stuff that day; she didn't even laugh like she usually did at Ashley and Lili squabbling over outfits.

Ashley decided to ignore A.A.'s sullen behavior. She didn't want anything to spoil her good mood. She was feeling so happy and benevolent these days, ever since that new blog had launched. The one everyone was talking about.

She knew there were rumors going around that the Ashleys were behind it—*as if!* They didn't need some anonymous computer nerd to tell them what they already knew, that they were seventh-grade royalty. AshleyRank was most likely started by some kind of fan of theirs—or else someone who was beyond desperate to be their friend.

Someone like Lauren Page. Lauren had spent the last few weeks sucking up to them, and this was yet another ploy to ingratiate herself into the group. It had to be her. First off, Lauren's father had made a nouveau-riche fortune when his video-sharing website YourTV went public over the summer. So obviously the Pages were techies. Two, that hot seventeen-year-old computer-whiz intern, Dex Bond—the one A.A. had been in love with for a minute—had plenty of time on his hands between driving Lauren to school and protecting her from imaginary kidnappers. (Who'd want to kidnap someone so boring? Hello!) Dex had probably created the blog in his spare time as a favor to the boss's sad-sack daughter.

In any case, AshleyRank was genius! Ashley liked any list that had her name at number one. And she especially liked any list that had everyone at Miss Gamble's talking. They even knew about it at Gregory Hall, and it was making the rounds at all the other private schools in the city. Yes! Today Miss Gamble's, tomorrow Page Six of the *New York Post*. Other girls planned their college applications. Ashley planned her future social life.

Ashley carefully stowed away her new clothes in one of the big Chanel shopping bags A.A.'s mother kept in the walk-in hall closet. Tri had said he'd walk her home, so she waved good-bye to the others and strolled out of the Fairmont with Tri gallantly carrying her bag. It wasn't far to her place, but she walked as slowly as possible, even though it had started raining again. She wanted to remember every detail of this afternoon. Because this was the moment.

The time was right for their first kiss.

Tri had been her boyfriend for a week now, if you counted the dance-with-death as the first day, despite the fact that she wasn't exactly conscious for all of it. They'd seen each other several times since the dance and sent each other approximately two hundred IMs.

He was perfect. He was sweet, he was polite, he was funny. When he looked into her eyes, she felt kind of crumbly and fluttery inside. She may have been the last of the Ashleys to get her period, but she was the first to have a *real* relationship with a boy, and not just some dumb online thing that didn't pan out, like A.A.'s so-called romance with "laxjock."

There was just one thing still bugging her.

Tri had never tried *once* to kiss her. Okay, so maybe it was because they'd only been going out for a week. Maybe he was just being shy. Maybe it was all part of being a gentleman— maybe they had etiquette lessons at Gregory Hall as well.

Gentlemanly was all well and good when you were, like, *ancient*, but right now she wanted him to step up to the plate and kiss her. If the other Ashleys started asking pointed questions, she was going to have to lie—and she hated lying. And lying about getting kissed was *très* lame. It made her feel like she was just pretending to have a boyfriend, like Lauren Page turning up at the mixer with Billy Reddy. Pretend boyfriends were so sixth grade!

Ashley surreptitiously looked at him from the corner of her eye. If he was too shy to kiss her, then she'd just have to take the initiative—make sure all systems were go. She'd heard that sometimes a girl had to make the move. Guys could be so clueless sometimes. The rain had petered out to a light drizzle, everything misty and romantic like in the movies. She couldn't have asked for better weather.

When they reached the tall wrought-iron gates of her house, she punched the security code into the little white box and waited for the gates to swing open.

"I guess I'll say good-bye here," said Tri, handing her the Chanel shopping bag.

"You can come in," she told him, trying to sound sultry and alluring. "Walk me to the door?"

There was no way she would let him kiss her on the street—in front of passing taxis and delivery trucks and random gardeners? Um. No. She'd been waiting for this all week.

She thought he'd kiss her when they'd snuggled up together at the movies, but he'd been way more interested in their shared tub of popcorn instead. When they'd met at Starbucks after school, the crowded coffeehouse didn't seem like the right moment for a make-out session either. This was the first time he was walking her home, and she'd planned it that way.

"C'mon," she said.

Tri hesitated and looked down at his shoes.

"Okay," he said finally, following her down the broad cobbled path that led to the double Spanish-style carved front doors.

Ashley walked in front of him so he could admire how cute she looked in her jeans and hoodie, swinging the Chanel bag nonchalantly. She set it down on the terra-cotta steps and turned to face him, taking care to stand on the path. There was no point in climbing the steps and making the difference in their height even worse.

"Are you sure you don't want to come in?" She wanted him to see their grand marble entryway, to know that her family was just as fabulous as his. Probably more fabulous, because both her parents had inherited massive trust funds, which meant nobody even *remembered* working in the Spencer household.

"I can't. I have to get home. I'll see you, okay? Maybe for brunch tomorrow?"

"Sure, but don't go yet," she whispered, not moving a muscle. She batted her eyelashes. Either he kissed her or he left her standing here. She wasn't going to be the one to walk away. "Come closer."

Tri's dark eyes looked anxious. "Why?"

"Because," Ashley breathed. Then she leaned toward

him, closing her eyes slowly. She knew how good she looked at that moment—how the dewy raindrops made her skin look pink and flushed, how her lips, softly parted, looked delicious. (She'd practiced in the mirror a thousand times.) He wouldn't be able to resist.

This was *it*.

He leaned toward her, and Ashley's mind whirred in jubilation. Yes! It was going to happen! She couldn't wait to tell all the other Ashleys how it all hap—

Huuuuhhh?

Tri wasn't kissing her. He was *hugging* her. And it was a squeeze-the-shoulders, friendly kind of hug. A five-second hug. The kind of hug you give cousins you haven't seen in eons, not a passionate embrace.

"See you," he called again, hurrying down the pathway toward the gates. Ashley watched him go, resisting the urge to stamp her foot. What kind of a boyfriend didn't kiss you?

She sighed and trudged up the steps. Whatever weirdness was going on in Tri's head was something she'd have to work out herself. No way was she going to discuss any of this with the other Ashleys. She had a reputation to maintain at all costs—the reputation of the girl ranked numero uno on AshleyRank. She may not have the perfect boyfriend, but at least, where it counted, she had the perfect score.

#1 ASHLEY SPENCER

STYLE: 10

Last seen at PlumpJack's Café in a to-die-for Chloé jacket and bubble dress that everyone immediately added to their shopping wish lists.

SOCIAL PRESENCE: 10

Adorable Boyfriend ("AB") completed the picture. The pair fed each other fries all morning. Aw, ain't young love sweet?

SMILE: 9

Practically glowing until AB accidentally spilled OJ all over bubble dress. Looked like she was leaning in for a kiss and they just missed each other. Cute!

SMARTS: 9

Maybe brunch isn't the best time to wear designer?

CUMULATIVE SCORE: 38

next >>

#2 ASHLEY "A.A." ALIOTO

STYLE: 10

Spotted down at the Marina, tanning on the lawn in a smokin' seashell bikini that made every other girl instantly look fat in their two-piece.

SOCIAL PRESENCE: 9

We admire a girl who can hang out on her own, although Ashley and her AB soon joined her.

SMILE: 7

Didn't look too happy to have company all of a sudden.

SMARTS: 9

A bikini in October? Global warming's not so bad after all!

CUMULATIVE SCORE: 35

#3 ASHLEY "LILI" LI

STYLE: 10

Seen at Saks as soon as it opened. Where on earth did she get those amazing curvy lace-up pumps??

SOCIAL PRESENCE: 8

Gracious to everyone at the store.

SMILE: 7

Although got a little upset when told they didn't have a certain Chloé leather jacket and bubble dress in stock.

SMARTS: 9

Who wears lace-up heels to go shopping?

CUMULATIVE SCORE: 34

4

WILL A SPOONFUL
OF SUGAR MAKE
THE SNOBERRY GO DOWN?

AUREN PAGE TOOK A DEEP BREATH AND WALKED toward the Ashleys' table. Strictly speaking, anyone could sit there. The tables in Miss Gamble's refectory (cafeteria was way too public school) were long and wooden, with room for at least fifteen people. But once the Ashleys were ensconced in the primo spot by the window, nobody dared to sit anywhere along the table, not even at the very end. Nobody wanted to be the butt of their relentless fashion analysis, and nobody wanted to risk annoying them.

Lauren had come pretty close herself to committing social suicide the week before the dance. She'd told the Ashleys *exactly* what she thought of them. Not much, as it turned out. The truth hurts and the truth was, it was a big mistake.

Once upon a time (just last year, actually), Lauren had been a fashion-challenged, work-study ugly duckling, but this semester, ever since her father had made unbelievable amounts of money, she had been transformed into a svelte, well-dressed, full-tuition-paying swan. A swan with a hidden agenda. To destroy the Ashleys.

She wanted to put an end to their reign of terror and make life better for everyone in the seventh grade. And the only way to do it was from the inside. She had to be part of the group if she wanted to rewrite the rules of the game. And rule number one was: play to their vanities.

She made her way to their table, carrying her tray of yogurt and spelt bread—Ashley's daily lunch, which was now the most popular option on the refectory's organic menu.

A few parents had voiced concern about the new item's super-low-fat quality (did it even have any real nutritional value?), but Lauren had overheard Ashley telling Lili that as far as she was concerned, the new spartan diet was a blessing in disguise for the student population. They could all stand to lose a few pounds!

As she stood in front of their table, Lauren could feel her ears turning red. She didn't have to turn around to know that the entire seventh-grade class was staring at her back. No one ever approached the Ashleys directly. And never at lunch.

Just a few weeks ago, Ashley herself had invited Lauren to

sit with them at their table. It had been a huge triumph, the likes of which had never been seen at Miss Gamble's. Sheridan Riley, famous for hero-worshipping the Ashleys, had once been allowed to lean against the wall next to the table, but that was as close as anyone else had ever gotten.

If Lauren had any hopes of returning to the head table, she'd have to prove herself worthy all over again. If she ended up slinking away, she could count on spending her entire year huddled in the library every lunch hour. And nothing at all would change.

Lauren glanced at a ragged group of misfits by the door. Would it hurt Ashley to stop making that Darth Vader breathing noise every time Cass Franklin walked by? Or for Lili to tell Daria Hart when the Honor Board was meeting, since Daria was a member? Or for A.A. to let Candace Yen actually play during a soccer match rather than just sit on the bench the whole time? Lauren knew what being invisible was like, and she wouldn't wish it on anybody.

Luckily, she had an ace up her sleeve. A foolproof plan to win back the Ashleys' friendship. The news she was about to spill was sure to get her a seat at this table every day of the week from now on. And once she had a seat at the table, maybe she could have a say in how things were run around here.

She cleared her throat.

Ashley Spencer raised an eyebrow, looked once at Lauren, and then turned back to Lili, as if Lauren wasn't even there. Lauren tried to exude confidence, even if the other two Ashleys didn't look too welcoming either.

"I . . . I have something to discuss with you all," she announced, her palms sweating as she held on to her tray. She glanced quickly at A.A., hoping to get a sort-of-friendly smile. Everyone always said that A.A. was the nicest of the Ashleys, but she was acting pretty stuck-up today, staring off into space as though she wanted to be somewhere else.

Lauren felt beads of sweat forming on her brow, and she was glad she had accessorized her uniform with a shrunken velvet blazer, black tights, and her high-heeled spectators. She might be doomed to outsider status, but at least she looked like an Ashley from the outside. She noticed they were all wearing colorful Pucci scarves tied around their necks.

"*You* have something to discuss?" Ashley asked, wrinkling her pert, freckle-free nose with distaste. "Is this, like, a committee meeting for some lame club we would never join?"

Lili glanced wryly at her.

"It's about a TV show," Lauren hurried to say. "A TV show we could be in."

"We?" asked Lili, suspicious but clearly interested.

Lauren nodded. This was the *hook*. . . .

But A.A. was still staring into space, twisting one of her

39

pigtails, and Ashley continued to look affronted, as though she couldn't believe that the interloper was presuming to set the agenda.

"You know how there's been a rumor going around that I'm going to star in my own reality show? Well, it's true—kind of. These guys my father met are producers at a new teen cable network, Sugar. Maybe you've heard about it?" Lauren asked, talking quickly. She was getting a little tired of standing, and the sixteen-ounce bottle of water was making her tray heavy.

"Oh yeah," said Lili, perking up a bit. "They make the *Boarding School Confidential* series, right? My sister's desperate for them to come to her school."

"Well, they've been talking to me about a show they're doing," Lauren told them. This was the *line*. . . .

"*You?*" Ashley asked, annoyed.

Lauren tried not to feel too insulted. "Yeah, but the thing is, it's not just me they want."

"Go on," Ashley said slowly, her blue eyes now fixed firmly on Lauren. Lili nodded, and even A.A. was paying attention now. "This is a reality show?"

Lauren nodded. "Yup. You know, with scripted scenarios, like *The Hills* or *Newport Harbor*."

"I *love* shows like that," gushed Lili. "Especially that one in Miami with the models."

"Or that one in soccer camp where everyone got kidnapped," added A.A., pushing away her tray of half-eaten lunch. "It took them three months to find them all."

"So . . . ?" Ashley prodded.

Lauren flipped her hair and took a sip from her water bottle before answering. "The producers want a group of girls. That's what I need to discuss with you today. Do you guys want to play my friends?" And that was the *sinker*. She held her breath. Would the Ashleys take the bait?

For a long moment, it looked as if Lauren would come up snake eyes, but then Ashley spoke. "You mean on television?"

"Us?" Lili asked.

"What do you mean 'play'?" A.A. wanted to know.

The Ashleys looked at one another. Lauren exhaled and shifted her weight from foot to foot. "I mean, if you don't want to, I can ask Melody and Olivia, or maybe Sheridan and her crew. . . ."

"Don't you dare," Lili said. They all looked at Ashley, who looked at Lauren, as if weighing her options.

"Sit down," Ashley ordered.

A.A. moved to the side to make room for Lauren.

Lauren climbed over the bench and lowered her body to the seat by the window. Success! Step One had been accomplished. Her fishing expedition had been successful; now she just had to keep reeling them in until she was one of them.

41

"Tell us more," Ashley demanded, her fork in the air. "Tell us everything."

Lauren gladly told them us much as she could. The show was called *Preteen Queen* and was scheduled to air as a midseason replacement for a karaoke show that had bombed. They were going to start taping episodes as early as next week if they could find the right girls. The girls who had originally been selected to do it had been fired when the producers discovered that two of them had been caught shoplifting over the summer.

"Serves them right," Lauren said with a laugh, digging into her salad and grimacing at its tastelessness. Tomorrow she would definitely bring her own sandwich instead of eating this crap. "Anyway, the producers are desperate to find the right girls, and my dad volunteered me. But it's supposed to be some kind of group thing, so I need a group."

"And you've found one." Ashley nodded, beaming like a Cheshire cat. "*Preteen Queen*. It's got the Ashleys written all over it, doesn't it?"

"Where do we sign?" joked A.A., drumming her Louboutin Mary Janes on the floor.

Lili had already whipped out her Blackberry. "When can we schedule the first meeting with the producers, Lo?" she asked Lauren.

And just like that, Lauren knew that once again she had her foot in the door. This time she hoped not to trip on it.

THERE'S BEEN A LOT OF MOVEMENT IN THE RANK THIS WEEK. Check out the latest stats and see how our girls are doing! Are your favorites still on top? Or are they about to lose their thrones? Here's one who's leapfrogged so high she still hasn't come down!

#10 LAUREN PAGE

STYLE: 8

Her successful promotion to the head table must be due to her stunning ensembles. Is that a school uniform or the Marc Jacobs fall line?

SOCIAL PRESENCE: 8

Confidence is key to social climbing, and she's as calm, cool, and collected as they come.

SMILE: 5

Only because she still doesn't do it often enough! L-Po, lighten up already, will ya?

SMARTS: 9

The only girl at school who's stopped eating the rabbit food they're serving at the ref. We like a girl who can think for herself.

CUMULATIVE SCORE: 30

WHAT'S FRENCH FOR "HOTTIE"?

AFTER SCHOOL A WEEK LATER, LILI'S DRIVER was waiting in her mother's black hybrid SUV. Lili always dreaded Monday afternoons, because she had to go straight from school to the Alliance Française to meet with her tutor. Once a week she had to spend an hour "enjoying" Advanced French conversation. She'd always hated French. She'd tried arguing her case with her mother, saying that Spanish would be a more useful language. After all, didn't their housekeeper, groundskeeper, and both nannies looking after her baby twin sisters all speak Spanish?

When Lili grew up, how was she expected to manage her staff if she wasn't fluent in their language? French was so *eighteenth century*. Unless she was planning to become an announcer at the Olympic Games or play the role of Mulan at Disneyland Paris, Lili didn't see why she had to suffer every

Monday afternoon. It didn't help that the only other student in her tutorial was some glaze-eyed surfer from Saint Aloysius, who was there to learn a few phrases before his parents took him on a vacation to Tahiti. He barely said a word, unless it was to ask the French words for "Big Kahuna" and "coral reef."

Whenever Lili tried to complain, her mother told her to focus on working for the United Nations or the State Department some day. What Lili didn't tell her achievement-obsessed mother, of course, was that her real dream was to run a nightclub in New York City. Well, maybe French could come in handy. She could call it the Moulin Rouge, she thought, gazing out of the tinted windows of the SUV as it passed a row of graceful Victorian mansions.

Lili's parents had their hearts on their daughter being the first Asian-American something—Supreme Court justice, Secretary of State, governor of California. She was expected to follow in her parents' footsteps and graduate from Harvard, of course. Actually, they expected her to go to Harvard twice—once for her bachelor's degree, and also for graduate school.

Maybe Harvard made you write your admissions essay in French, Lili thought, her heart sinking at the sight of the cream-colored Alliance Française building, with its neat blue shutters and pristine window boxes, the French flag hanging above the front door waving in the stiff breeze.

But it was hard to be too glum today because of the news Lauren Page had sprung at lunch. Their own reality TV show! Now that was the kind of after-school activity that Lili could get enthused about. She had already cleared a number of windows in her overpacked schedule, and Lauren had promised to call the producers that afternoon to set up the first meeting. They wanted to start filming right away, Lauren had said, because the first episodes of the show would go on air while it was still in production.

The only thing that worried her was the prospect of Ashley trying to take over the show. That would be *so* like her. Ashley couldn't be content with being number one on AshleyRank, or having a boyfriend, or stealing the best outfit at A.A.'s place from under Lili's nose, or any of her other—let's face it—not-totally-deserved accolades and accomplishments.

There was no doubt in Lili's mind: Ashley was already fitting the *Preteen Queen* crown for her blond head. Lili had to make sure that didn't happen, and the first place she planned to start was with Lauren herself. The closer Lili got to Lauren, the more camera time she'd score. As soon as she got home tonight, in the half hour free she had once a day, Lili was going to execute her plan.

She slammed the heavy door of the SUV and marched up the steps of the Alliance Française. She announced herself in

French to the pretty receptionist at the desk, then walked up the dramatic, curving staircase to the second-floor private library. She arrived to find her tutor, Madame LeBrun, waiting for her in the elegant, wood-paneled room, seated in a wingback armchair and looking even more thin and pallid than last week.

"Bonjour, Madame," Lili said, demurely sitting in a chair and stowing her Fendi Spy bag at her feet.

The French teacher sniffed, pressing a delicate handkerchief to her pointy nose. She had allergies all year round, apparently. She wore a drab gray cardigan over a matching jersey skirt, the collar of her blouse was askew.

Lili shuddered. What about that famous French style? Why wasn't Madame LeBrun wearing an Hermès scarf or a Chanel suit? At least she could have a chic purse—but no. Madame always carried a canvas book bag overflowing with papers and books. It wasn't even a cute canvas bag with her initials embroidered on it, like the one from L.L. Bean that Lili's dad liked to take on their boat. She was sure that if her mother ever got a look at Madame LeBrun, Nancy Khan would demand an instant refund.

Lili looked around for the only other student in the tutorial. "Is it just the two of us?"

"En francais, s'il vous plaît," said Madame LeBrun.

Lili posed her question in the correct language.

47

"Greg est allé à Tahiti," Madame began to say, but before she could finish, a giant sneeze overtook her bony frame. She screwed up her face, gesturing at Lili with her white handkerchief, then hurried out of the room in a flurry of minisneezes.

Lili sighed. If Greg was already surfing his brains out, it was unlikely that he would return to class. Unless his parents were plotting to ski at Val d'Isère over Christmas, his days of French conversation were probably over.

The door swung open again, and Lili heaved another long sigh. She'd hoped Madame would take longer to blow her nose, dab at her watering eyes, and recover her Gallic composure. However, she registered quickly that it wasn't Madame. It was a boy. A slim boy in faded corduroys and a worn flannel shirt, shouldering a scuffed backpack and holding on to a dented skateboard. A boy with fair hair, dark eyes, and an appealingly sleepy grin. Lili's heart started flip-flopping around.

"Hey," he said, dropping into the chair next to Lili. "Is this the French conversation class?" His voice was low and scratchy-sounding, as if he'd just woken up.

She nodded, suddenly unable to speak. She glanced shyly up at him from behind her textbook.

"Max Costa," he said coolly, holding out his hand.

"Ashley Li," squeaked Lili, trying to stay calm. She

cleared her throat and shook his hand, her skin tingling at the contact. "Everyone calls me Lili."

"Gotcha."

She beamed at him. Max was definitely of the scruffy-hottie variety and looked a bit like a bad boy. The kind her mom always warned her away from, which piqued Lili's interest even more. She was tired of listening to her mom.

"You're taking French?" she asked.

"*Oui*, unfortunately," Max replied. "I flunked it last semester, so my parents are on my butt to raise my grade. I'd have been here weeks earlier, but I had to bow out of soccer first." Big sigh. "It's not too bad. I still get to play lacrosse."

Lili learned that Max was in seventh grade at Reed Prep, the coed private school across town that was known for its "alternative" policies—kids were clumped into "progress groups" instead of grades, teachers were called by their first names, and students could wear whatever they wanted because there was no dress code. Miss Gamble's girls weren't supposed to date Reed Prep boys out of loyalty to their brother school Gregory Hall, but Lili could see herself making an exception for him. He was capital-C cute.

"You go to Miss Gamble's?" he asked, noting the uniform.

"Uh-huh."

"Didn't someone almost die at the dance the other week?"

Ugh. It was so annoying how Ashley's near demise was such big news that even kids who didn't go to their school had heard of it.

"Yeah, but she's completely fine now." Lili wanted to get the conversation away from Ashley and back onto herself. The others were going to *freak* when they found out she was taking a private class with a totally crushable boy every Monday. What was she thinking? She *j'adored* French!

"That's good." Max nodded. He smiled at her and looked as if he was going to say something more, but didn't. The silence made Lili feel a tad uncomfortable, and she rested her chin on her hand and began twirling her fountain pen on her fingers to calm her nerves.

When her phone began ringing suddenly, she startled and fumbled with the pen, smudging ink all over her cheek.

"Oops!" She turned red as she wiped her face with the palm of her hand and tried to answer her phone at the same time. Max was going to think she was the biggest klutz! So much for coming across as cool.

"What is it?" she snapped into her phone. It was Lauren. "Slow down! You're talking so fast, you're hyper. That's better. You just bumped into Billy Reddy? Okay, so?"

Billy Reddy was a gorgeous high school sophomore, star of the Gregory Hall lacrosse team, and a member of the wealthiest and most talked-about family in San Francisco.

Half the girls at Miss Gamble's were in love with Billy, and the Ashleys used to stalk him walking back from school every day. But though Lauren had brought him to the dance, it was pretty obvious that she wasn't his girlfriend. Lili was a Billy groupie too, although sneaking another covert glance at Max, as she vainly tried to cover up the ink on her skin, she wasn't sure how long that was going to last. Besides, Billy was in high school—way too old.

Apparently Lauren had promised Billy earlier that she would bring a huge cheering section from Miss Gamble's to the lax semifinals, which somehow had become a promise to provide cheerleaders for the game as well, since Gregory Hall was all-boys.

"Help!" Lauren said. "I think he thinks I'm going to have some kind of halftime show or something!"

"A halftime show at the lacrosse game?" Lili asked, hoping she didn't have some kind of ink Hitler mustache on her face.

"You're talking about the big lacrosse matchups next weekend?" Max asked. "Sorry, I couldn't help but overhear. We're playing Greg Hall then, in the junior high division. Are you going?" He gave her a breathtaking smile.

Lili thought fast. "Don't worry about a thing," she told Lauren. "We'll do something special. The Ashleys made nationals in dance team last year, you know." Before Lauren

51

could reply, Lili had hung up the phone. She turned to Max. "I wouldn't dream of missing it."

"Excellent!" said Max, his face lighting up.

So what if she had no time at all in her schedule to practice a dance routine? She would make time. Especially if it meant that Max would get a chance to see her in a cute little outfit and see how truly coordinated she was.

By the time Madame came back to the room, an idea was forming in her mind. She had to meet with the producers to see if they'd buy it, but she was sure she could talk them into it. She smiled. If the plan worked, it would shove Ashley out of the limelight—once and for all.

FRIENDLY FOURSOME OR VIPER'S NEST? THAT'S JUST REALITY (TELEVISION)

THE LOBBY OF THE CLIFT HOTEL IN DOWN-town San Francisco was a stunning room that featured soaring double-height ceilings, etched Venetian mirrors, billowing white velvet curtains, and cheeky interpretations of classic furniture—a Louis Quinze chair in plastic, say, or a chandelier made out of twigs instead of crystal.

Ashley had been here many times before, usually to eat with her parents or grandparents in the clubby, elegant Redwood Room. Once her family had stayed here for three days when work was being done to the exterior of their house and her parents decided they had to get away from the noise and chaos.

They would have taken Ashley out of school and gone

down to a chic B and B on the coast near Big Sur, or to the Auberge du Soleil in Napa Valley, but she had exams that week and needed to be somewhere close to Miss Gamble's. Living in a hotel was fine—A.A. certainly liked it, but then she'd never known anything else. But Ashley had been glad to get home to their airy, spacious mansion overlooking the Golden Gate Bridge. Hotels were so . . . *public*. Anyone could wander in and out, or just sit in the lobby wearing white sweat socks and reading *USA Today*, and nobody could do anything about it. Not even the fashionable staff at the Clift.

The producers of *Preteen Queen* were waiting for them in the hotel's living room, and Ashley made sure to stick close by Trudy Page, Lauren's mother, so that she'd get introduced first. Well, after Lauren, but that was only fair: This show was Lauren's thing. For now. Ashley had every intention of making sure the cameras were pointed *her* way as often as possible.

To Ashley's surprise, the producers weren't old and boring at all. In fact, they dressed more like college students than television executives. They were even younger than her parents, Ashley guessed. The female producer was Tiffany, a friendly-looking Asian girl in trim black pants and a fitted shirt, clutching a bulging leather Filofax.

The two guys were Matt and Jasper, both in T-shirts and jeans and somewhat interchangeable, with their shaggy hair and five o' clock shadows. Matt laid his laptop open on the marble-top coffee table, clambering to his feet to shake their hands. Jasper had a British accent, which seemed to make the whole meeting even more exciting. Mrs. Page was acting like he was Orlando Bloom, gushing over him like a besotted fan.

Ashley's parents were embarrassing sometimes, like when they kissed each other in public, or when her father played his Phish records when her friends were over. But they had nothing on Lauren's mother, their self-appointed driver and chaperone. She was dressed like an extra in *Pirates of the Caribbean*, her hair tied with a gaudy bandanna, her white shiny stretch pants too tight, and her gold leather sandals laced tightly around her plump ankles.

The Pages had only been rich for about the last five minutes, and Mrs. Page hadn't learned yet that you shouldn't buy everything you see in a *Vogue* Versace ad and wear it all at once.

"Shall I order tea?" Trudy asked Jasper in what sounded like a quasi-British accent of her own, and Ashley raised her eyebrows at A.A., sitting on the other side of the table next to Tiffany. Lauren must have noticed: She flushed bright pink. Ashley would have felt sorry for her, but why bother? Lauren should be grateful the Ashleys were there at all, willing to be pretend-friends with her. Without them, her show would be canceled after one episode.

"I've already asked for iced teas for everyone—is that okay?" Tiffany said with a smile, cracking open her giant organizer. "I know we all have a time crunch, so we should get down to business right away."

"Of course," said Ashley, giving Tiffany her friendliest smile.

Tiffany told them the concept of the show: five groups of friends in five big cities, competing to be the "Preteen Queen" of their hometown.

"What do you mean compete?" Lauren asked. "My dad didn't say anything about the show being a competition."

"Yeah, is it like *America's Got Talent* or something?" said A.A., who didn't look too excited about that aspect either. "I thought it was supposed to be like *The Hills*."

"It is like *The Hills*," Jasper said soothingly. "That's why we wanted a group of friends—we wanted to show what life as a tween is really like, all the highs, the lows, the laughter, and the drama."

"The catfights, you mean," said Lili wisely.

"We like to think of it as creating tension," Matt put in, grinning.

"And who decides the winner?" Ashley asked, her mind already racing to figure out how to slay her rivals—er, her friends.

"The audience, of course," Tiffany told them. "The first five episodes will showcase a group of girls in five different cities. After each show, the audience votes. Only one girl from each city will be selected to go on to the next round.

"The five winners will be flown out to live in a penthouse in New York for two weeks to battle it out for the national title. Whoever wins gets a contract with a top talent agent, a publicist, a once-in-a-lifetime shopping spree, and the cover of *Teen Vogue*."

New York City! It was Ashley's dream to live in New York, especially with a team ready to take her to the social and celebrity stratosphere.

"Only one of us can get through?" Ashley's mind was whirring.

"Unfortunately." Jasper laughed. "I hope it doesn't come between your friendships. It's only a game, yes?"

"Right," A.A. mumbled, while Lili looked as intense as Ashley had ever seen her and Lauren bit her nails.

Lauren hadn't been exaggerating. The producers wanted to start taping right away, and they had already approached Miss Gamble's for permission to film an Honor Board meeting the following week.

"But the only one of us on the Honor Board is Lili," Ashley pointed out, and Lili gave her a cat-who-swallowed-the-cream smile. Lil was acting very smug all of a sudden, and Ashley realized that Lili had probably one-upped her and called the producers even before the meeting. Ashley wouldn't put it past her. She had to make sure Lili wouldn't get filmed on her own turf, hello.

"I've got a better idea," Ashley said, fixing her wide-eyed gaze on Jasper, the look she used on her father whenever she wanted to buy something too expensive or possibly age-inappropriate. "I've been planning something special for our class, and the four of us are having our first meeting about it on Thursday. You could film that."

"The four of you?" Matt sounded eager. "That would be great. What is it?"

Ashley ignored the puzzled looks A.A. and Lili were shooting her.

"It's a . . . um, it's a Friendship Ceremony," she faltered. *Quick, Ashley—think.* "I've been talking to Miss Charm about it, and she loves the idea," she lied.

"That's our Manners and Morals teacher," Lili explained, and when the producers all looked blank she went on, "She teaches etiquette. It's our first class on Mondays and Thursdays."

"Sorry to be slow, but what does this Friendship Ceremony entail exactly?" asked Jasper.

"It's a celebration of friendship." Ashley fluttered her long lashes in his direction. She felt like patting herself on the back. The producers wanted friendship drama, didn't they? Well, she would give it to them. In spades.

"Miss Charm wanted us to find a way of creating some new traditions at Miss Gamble's, and I came up with this." Ashley began outlining her idea.

"I don't remember . . . ," Lauren began, and then stopped herself. Ashley smiled: Lauren was learning fast. You should *never* admit to not knowing something, because that just told everyone else what an out-of-the-loop loser outsider you were. A.A. and Lili didn't know anything about this either—mainly because Ashley was making it up on the spot—but they weren't drawing attention to themselves. They'd learned to go along with whatever Ashley wanted, anyway.

"But doesn't Miss Gamble's have a policy against cliques?" asked Lauren a little sharply, when Ashley was done describing her awesome idea. Ashley bristled. Lauren must have forgotten the importance of being a team player. Maybe she wasn't such a fast learner after all.

"Yeah," said Lili, her pretty face troubled. She placed her glass of iced tea carefully on its ivory paper coaster. "I don't know if Miss Charm is going to like that idea very much."

Lili could be such a goody-goody sometimes.

"She'll like it. She likes anything I suggest," Ashley said. "I could turn the whole class against her in a second."

"I wish we were filming right now. I can tell you guys are the arbiters of what's in and out at school," Jasper observed with a wry smile.

"Exactly." Ashley brushed a hank of blond hair away from her face. "Once in a while we get into a *little* trouble, mainly because girls are so jealous of us. That kind of thing happens a lot when you're as popular as we are."

"Well," said Jasper, shaking his head and grinning at Lauren, "I can see why you girls are the right ones for our show."

Lauren said nothing and gave an embarrassed half smile. Maybe she was upset that the Ashleys were running *her* show. She should just deal. Last semester, the only person Lauren hung out with carried an oxygen tank instead of a Fendi handbag.

"That's why the Friendship Ceremony is brilliant! We'll be promoting unity among the class," Ashley said, not even bothering to look at Lili. What was up with her? Ashley had come up with a save-the-day brainwave and Lili was trying to sabotage it!

"It sounds perfect," said Tiffany. "And the four of you are best friends, right?"

Ashley nodded. One by one, the other girls followed suit, Lauren nodding too. Ashley figured that was all right for now. After all, they had agreed to play Lauren's BFFs for TV.

"We just need to get permission from the school to film that, of course," Jasper said.

"Oh, you'll get permission," Ashley reassured him.

She'd make sure of it. Even if her father had to finance a new library wing for Miss Gamble's, she was going to get those cameras into that classroom on Thursday. As far as she was concerned, *Preteen Queen* was now *The Ashley Show.*

7

YES, THEY THINK THEY CAN DANCE

.A. ARRIVED AT DANCE-TEAM REHEARSAL on time—four o'clock on Wednesday, just as Lili had asked, although it was a pretty last-minute request, especially for Lili. Ashley and Lili were both driving her crazy with their secret plans. First Ashley sprang her "Friendship Ceremony" idea on everyone at the *Preteen Queen* meeting yesterday, and now Lili had decided they needed to come up with a special routine for the big lacrosse semis next week.

Why those games were so special all of a sudden, A.A. did not know. To be honest, she was kind of tired of boys. Between Ashley cooing over Tri and Lili gushing over some Reed Prep stud in her French class, A.A. was feeling like a total spinster.

She had nothing romantic to look forward to right now—nothing. By the time she'd figured out that her secret online love, laxjock, was probably Tri, he was already smitten with Ashley, asking her to dance, feeding her (okay, unwittingly) nut-infested cupcakes, and then waltzing off into the sunset with her.

Not that she cared. It was only Tri. They were just friends, and she didn't think of him in any other way. She just couldn't believe he actually liked Ashley. A.A. liked Ashley too—she was a lot of fun and surprisingly sweet underneath all the snobbery—but she never imagined Tri falling for someone so . . . superficial.

Rehearsal today was in the Little Theater, a multi-use space that was part auditorium and part gym. A.A. busied herself with yoga stretches. If all else failed, working out always helped clear her head.

A few minutes later Lili bustled in with an entire entourage—Tiffany, one of the producers from the day before; several cameramen; a boom operator; a sound guy; two production assistants wielding clipboards; and someone else whose job seemed to be holding all the power cords. Lili looked exuberant, and behind her was Lauren, walking just as briskly.

Both had changed out of their school uniforms. Lili was wearing Y3 Adidas head to toe, while Lauren unzipped her Juicy velour hoodie to reveal a body-hugging lycra top and blue Title Nine cutoff Pilates pants.

"What's going on?" A.A. asked.

"They're filming us!" said Lili.

"Yeah, I can see that. Why?"

"I told them that after-school activities are a normal part of a preteen's life, and they wanted to capture it," Lili explained, as if it made perfect sense.

"But I thought they weren't going to start filming until the Friendship Ceremony meeting," said A.A., still confused. "And where's Ashley?"

Lili blithely ignored A.A.'s questions as she stretched her hamstrings. A.A. would have liked to get to the bottom of it, but the sound guy was waiting to put a mike on her, and she didn't want to appear uncooperative.

"Coach is just parking," Lili called, dropping her cell phone into her bag. "Tiffany, you're going to *love* him. He gives good TV."

A.A. nodded as she clipped the microphone to her jogging bra. "Trent's a total Carson." It looked like Lili was running the show, and she wasn't about to get in the way.

The heavy door clanged open and A.A. looked up, expecting to see Ashley in her usual rehearsal gear—a pale blue one-piece with a gray cashmere shrug. But instead a very tall, very gay guy in his thirties, with a shaved head, dressed in gray sweatpants and a white muscle tee, bounded into the room.

"Hello, Lady Miss Ashleys!" he called, clapping his hands. "Miss Lili, where is my entrance music? Gimme the beat!"

"Just getting it ready!" Lili bent over the CD player, cuing up a disco remix of Diana Ross's "I'm Coming Out." "Tiffany, Lauren, everybody, this is Trent, our coach. He's a trainer at Crunch, a former backup dancer for Paula Abdul, and a five-time national dance-team champion."

"And a former pageant queen, but we won't get into that now," said Trent, accepting his microphone gladly and sticking the receiver into the waist of his sweatpants. "How do I look?" he purred, throwing kisses at the camera.

Trent stopped mugging long enough to notice Lauren's presence. "And who are you?"

"She's a new member of the team," Lili said quickly.

"I'm Lauren, a big fan of your work on 'Cold Hearted.'" Lauren smiled, extending a hand. "Next to you, Paula looks like a dancing dwarf."

Trent looked charmed immediately. "Oh, go on." He blushed. Then he pursed his lips. "But where is Miss Ashley?"

Nobody knew.

"Should we have left her a message?" Lauren was asking, but Lili shushed her as Trent clapped his hands to get their attention.

"Now, in a line please, *tout de suite*. Let's see your moves."

"We're not going to wait for Ashley?" A.A. asked Lili. It was aggravating to be waiting around all the time for Ashley, but it seemed strange to start rehearsing without her. And how were they going to work Lauren into this new routine?

"I don't think so," said Lili breezily. "She's so busy getting ready for the presentation tomorrow, she may not even show—I don't really know."

Lili was lying, A.A. could tell. Maybe she hadn't even told Ashley about this rehearsal: A.A. wouldn't put it past Lili. After the meeting with the producers yesterday, things were strangely tense between Ashley and Lili. The show seemed to have ramped up their usual competitiveness times ten. How Lili hoped to keep all this from Ashley, A.A. didn't know. Wasn't everything going to be on television? But it wasn't her problem. Let Lili take the flak when Ashley found out they were rehearsing behind her back. All A.A. wanted to do was get her dance on.

She looked up and out of the floor-length windows of the Little Theater. She thought she'd noticed someone lurking by the curtains. Ashley? But why wouldn't she just join the rehearsal?

"Enough chatting, Miss Thang!" Trent turned his back to them and clicked his fingers. "I'm going to go through the steps and then we'll try it with music. Repeat after me!"

66

By the time Trent decided, a few minutes later, that they were ready for music—a cool old-school techno song, Shannon's "Let the Music Play," because he said it would get those lacrosse players "all worked up"—two things had happened.

First, A.A. had completely forgotten to be self-conscious in front of the cameras, because she was enjoying herself so much learning all the new moves and grooving to the lyrics of the dance-team warm-up *("He's dancing his way back to me . . . he's dancing his way back to me . . .")*. Somehow the image of Tri came to mind, but she tried to shake it off. And second, Lili had pointed out, in a silky and smug voice, that Lauren's inexperience was showing, so it would be better if she herself danced in the middle of the group.

In other words, in Ashley's usual place.

This is going to be interesting, thought A.A.

LAUREN DISCOVERS THE
CAMERA ADDS TEN POUNDS . . .
OF DRAMA

WHEN DEX DROPPED LAUREN OFF IN her father's silver Bentley Continental the next morning, he had a few words of caution. "Take it easy," he said, motioning to the satellite truck parked outside the school with the Sugar cable network's pastel logo on the side door. "Don't get too caught up in all that crap now. Remember, you shouldn't care so much what other people think. You're great the way you are."

"Dex, it's *me*," Lauren assured him with a grin. "You know I think reality TV is totally bogus. Don't worry."

This was not the Lauren of just over a month ago, who had been so nervous about coming back to school she'd almost puked during the morning car ride. No, this Lauren was ready for battle.

Sure, she'd taken a little more care with her appearance than usual, meticulously flat-ironing her chestnut shoulder-length hair, applying a deeper shade of lip gloss since she'd read that makeup had to be more dramatic when one was in front of the camera, and selecting a gorgeous ruffled silk shirt to wear with the uniform skirt instead of the mandatory button-down. But that was only because yesterday afternoon she hadn't had time to beautify since Lili had sprung the cameras on them at the last minute, so she wanted to look extra good today.

And for the first time this semester, she wasn't wearing her high-heeled black-and-white spectator pumps. She'd called Ashley last night and told her that while *Preteen Queen* was filming, she thought she should wear a pair of red-soled Louboutin Mary Janes like them. She'd even bought a matching Pucci scarf as well, to complete the picture. Just on filming days, of course. Ashley had agreed it was a great idea.

Lauren was gratified. Maybe if she pressed hard enough, the Ashleys would forget they were only *pretending* to be friends.

Instead of going straight into class, Lauren made a beeline for the bench by the playground where the Ashleys held court before school each day. They were there as usual: A.A. on Ashley's right, Lili on Ashley's left, doing their usual before-school fashion-and-hair scrutiny.

If she was worried about what Lili or A.A. would say about her copycat shoes and scarf, she needn't have been. Neither of them raised an eyebrow.

"Oh my God," said Ashley. "Did you *see* Guinevere Parker? Those earmuffs she's wearing make her bizarro bobblehead even larger. It's not even winter and she's already dressing like a yeti!"

"I don't know, it is kind of cold," Lauren said softly.

"Whatever. It's sixty degrees. When is it not sixty degrees in San Francisco?" Ashley harrumphed. She took a sip from her chai latte and nudged Lili. "Look! Cass Franklin's doing the Michael Jackson again!" True enough, the poor girl was wearing a white hospital mask over the lower half of her face, just like the weirdo pop star. The three Ashleys dissolved into hysterics, and Lauren attempted a laugh but didn't have the heart for it.

"They're going to film us here at recess," Lili said, changing the subject.

"Hey, Lauren, did you get your notes last night?" A.A. leaned forward. They'd all been sent "talking points" to keep them on track. The producers wanted them to discuss what they had planned for the "Friendship Ceremony."

"Yeah, easy enough. I think I have it all down." Lauren nodded. Truth be told, she didn't have a lot of lines. She could already see where this show was headed, and the producers had already written her off as the boring, nice one. Not that she minded too much—she was only using the show to get in with the Ashleys so she could take them down one day.

"Remember," said Ashley, smiling at her in a shark-about-to-devour-goldfish way, "I'm the one who's going to make the presentation to the rest of the class this morning. This whole ceremony is my idea, after all."

Lili nodded serenely. Lauren figured out that Ashley didn't know about the secret dance-team practice that had also been taped for the show. Boy, was Ashley in for a surprise. Lauren would love to see her face when she found out.

The whole dance-team routine for the lacrosse game was so out of left field. Billy Reddy had mentioned to Dex that Lauren had promised to rustle up some screaming girls for the game, and it had snowballed into some kind of cheerleader extravaganza. She was amused that Lili had taken it so deeply to heart, although she had to admit she was a bit excited to perform in front of so many boys as well.

Ashley was taking apart Olivia DeBartolo's disastrous new fur hat when the second bell rang and it was time to dash up the stairs and take their seats in etiquette class. When they filed into the classroom in the front of the mansion, Lauren noticed that the same crew who'd filmed them at the dance-team practice had already set up for the new location. There were even more people this time—Jasper and Matt were both there with walkie-talkies, and Tiffany was talking to one of the lighting guys about the how stained-glass windows would affect their shot.

Miss Charm was completely flustered, and also over-dressed, wearing a peach mock-Chanel jacket with matching kilt and a crystal brooch the size of a large apple. She had much more makeup on than usual as well, Lauren noticed, and every time she moved her head, dustlike powder flew off her face.

Ashley made a big deal about getting miked up, and Lauren had to repress a grin, since she and the other Ashleys were old pros. Filming was a lot more boring and stop-and-start than yesterday, however. Matt and Jasper were a lot more micromanaging than Tiffany had been. Matt asked Miss Charm to make her introductory speech three times before they were happy with the sound and the light. By the time Ashley got up to announce the Friendship Ceremony, class was almost half over.

Ashley explained the details of the Friendship Ceremony, sounding as if she were addressing the White House press corps. "Everyone will divide into groups, and then each group will work on a little presentation. Each group will make a banner representing their group, and everyone will stand up and say why they like each other."

"Plus, each group has to sing a song, a theme song for their group," Lili chimed in from the front row. Ashley's beauty-queen smile sagged for a second with annoyance.

"I was just getting to that," Ashley said in a frosty voice. "Everyone has to choose a song about friendship and then sing it to the whole class."

"Can we bring in music?" asked Sheridan Riley.

"No," Ashley said firmly. Lauren knew why: Ashley had a strong, clear singing voice and had no trouble singing in tune. A lot of the other girls would struggle without a CD playing in the background to help them out.

Overall, the idea went down pretty well. Some of the girls were muttering that they had only a week to get their presentations together, and some of the less popular girls were looking desperately around the room, wondering whose group might let them in. But nobody was going to rebel against a plan initiated by the Ashleys. And who wanted to look like a friendless whiner when there were TV cameras filming every word?

At recess, after her honors science class, Lauren returned to the bench to find Matt and his cameras already set up and all the Ashleys preening with hairbrushes and lip gloss before filming began again. Even A.A. was fixing her pigtails and checking her reflection in her iPhone.

Matt told them to start talking about their banner, and

Ashley, of course, the good little soldier she was, rushed to be the first one to speak.

"So we should use canvas instead of paper, naturally," she insisted. "That way we can sew or staple our items on and make it three-di—"

"I already thought of that," interrupted Lili, pulling a portfolio out from under the bench. "Here are some designs that I had put together."

"These are great, Lili," Lauren gushed, even though it wasn't her turn to speak. She knew that if she complimented Lili's designs, it would annoy Ashley.

"Yeah," Ashley said flatly, giving the portfolio a cursory examination. "But I think we need to go in a different direction—I was thinking of bringing in some professional expertise."

"What do you mean?" Lili asked, looking affronted.

"You wouldn't cut your own hair, would you?" Ashley asked. "You'd leave it to Frédéric Fekkai. Well. I don't think we should design our own banner."

Lili looked as if it was the most obnoxious thing she'd ever heard, and Lauren had to agree. Besides, wasn't that cheating? But maybe not, since they wouldn't be graded on the activity.

"What kind of item do you want to represent you?" A.A. asked, determined to stick to her talking points.

It wasn't clear who exactly A.A. was speaking to, and both Lili and Ashley started talking at once. Ashley, who had the louder voice, won.

"A violin for Lili, I thought—we could have a miniature made up in rosewood. And I'd have a crystal tiara. Because, well, you know." Ashley smiled up at the camera.

"No, I don't." Lauren feigned ignorance. "Why a tiara?" She wanted to show exactly how vain and pompous Ashley could be.

But Ashley only smiled.

"You guys! I don't want a violin," argued Lili, jostling to open her portfolio. "That's so dorky!" She frowned. "I was thinking, for me, a Blackberry. I can get a faux one stitched in black leather. It'll look really cool. Or maybe I could get, like, a pair of scales to represent how I'm on Honor Board."

Ashley made a twirling motion with her finger to indicate "big whoop."

"Why do you always diss Honor Board?" Lili asked, sounding incredibly whiny.

"I'm not," Ashley said, giving Lili an unexpected hug. "You know I'm just teasing, Brainiac."

"What about you, A.A.?" Lauren asked, a bit disappointed that Ashley had backed off a prima donna scuffle.

"I don't know," said A.A., scuffing one toe in the grass. "Maybe something sporty."

Ashley crinkled her nose.

"How about, like, a pair of long legs? They're your best feature," Lili suggested.

"Or a big pair of pink lips," Ashley offered.

"Why?" A.A. was bemused.

"You know, because you've kissed all these boys," Ashley said wickedly.

Ouch, Lauren thought.

"No, I haven't!" A.A. protested.

"How many boys have you kissed?" Lili asked, sounding innocent but obviously seeing an opportunity to dump on A.A. as well. Votes were on the line, after all, although Lauren wasn't sure if this was the right way to get them.

"I don't know . . . ," A.A. said miserably, trying not to look at the camera. "Not that many . . ."

"Let's review, shall we?" Ashley held up her hand and started checking off with her fingers. "At that high school party you went to, didn't you make out with a freshman from Saint Aloysius? In fact, it was two boys, wasn't it? You made out with both of them, and one of them stalked you afterward, remember?"

"Totally!" said Lili, nudging Lauren. A.A.'s cheeks were pink, and Lauren couldn't help but feel sorry for her. Ashley was really acting up for the cameras.

"And don't forget your online Romeo—laxjock. Did he

turn out to be a freak, or did you kiss him, too?" Lili asked.

"You guys, you know I didn't meet up with anyone. I was right there at the dance when you collapsed," A.A. said quietly.

"Oh, that's right." Ashley sighed. "When I collapsed and almost died because Lili had promised to supply nut-free cupcakes and then went back on her word."

"I didn't do it on purpose!" Lili protested. "I didn't even know you had an allergy. Why do you have to keep bringing this up?"

"I don't know. Maybe because I *nearly died* or something?"

The bell rang for third period, and Matt clapped his hands.

"This is great, girls," he said. Lauren couldn't agree more. "You're all naturals. Next week at the Friendship Ceremony, we want you to perform last."

By the time Lauren got to her next class, she felt invigorated. If this was all it took to make the Ashleys look ridiculous, then she could just sit back, relax, and enjoy the show.

#1 ASHLEY SPENCER

STYLE: 10

Spotted leaving the offices of Chiat\Day (a famous design and advertising firm) with a fat pink linen portfolio bound with a suede strap and "The Ashleys" embossed on the front.

SOCIAL PRESENCE: 10

Spies tell us she bossed around the design team with her usual élan.

SMILE: 9

Didn't look too happy to find out it would be a six-week turnaround on her Friendship Ceremony banner.

SMARTS: 10

Offered the team triple the fee if they got it done faster. Banner production confirmed!

CUMULATIVE SCORE: 39   (Hey, no one is perfect!)

#2 ASHLEY "A.A." ALIOTO

STYLE: 10

Fills out an Adidas by Stella McCartney jog bra and leggings like no one else can.

SOCIAL PRESENCE: 8

Kept her cool when she noticed crazy boy stalker from last semester has resurfaced and was peeking in on dance-team practice.

SMILE: 10

Looked positively ecstatic when crazy stalker beat it after dance coach scared him away.

SMARTS: 9

Maybe next time should think twice before kissing two boys at Truth or Dare.

CUMULATIVE SCORE: 37

next >>

#3 ASHLEY "LILI" LI

STYLE: 10

Looked especially chic arriving for French

conversation on Monday afternoon.

SOCIAL PRESENCE: 10

We gotta admit, she's got a certain *je ne sais quoi*!

SMILE: 7

Wheezing French professor keeps inserting herself

in conversations made for two.

SMARTS: 9

Kudos to a girl who can flirt in two languages!

CUMULATIVE SCORE: 36

#9 LAUREN PAGE

STYLE: 9

Speaks softly but carries a Prada handbag.

SOCIAL PRESENCE: 9

From head lunch table to the Bench of Judgment
in a week! Who knows how high this one is going to go?

SMILE: 6

Current bemused expression an improvement on
look of total anxiety.

SMARTS: 8

Aligning with the Ashleys is the smartest move
she's made.

CUMULATIVE SCORE: 32

LILI HAS A SECOND CHANCE
TO MAKE A GOOD
FIRST IMPRESSION

"SO HOW ARE YOU FEELING RIGHT NOW?" The production intern was holding a microphone just off camera, and Lili made sure to talk slowly to be understood. It was halftime at the Gregory Hall–Saint Aloysius varsity lacrosse game, and in a few minutes Lili would be out there dancing her butt off for the crowd. Right now they were taping a "confessional" for the reality show. Jasper had explained that since they weren't going to mike them up during the performance but tape them from afar, they wanted to get their thoughts on the action beforehand.

"I'm really pumped. I like seeing hard work pay off," she said.

The day was gray and rainy and the game was tied at four

all. Saint A's had managed to bus in dozens of cheering supporters, but only half of the upper-form girls from Miss Gamble's had bothered to show up.

Standing in a muddy field didn't sound like a great way to spend a Saturday afternoon, even with the promise of boy watching. To muster interest, Lili had started a rumor that the person behind AshleyRank would be revealed at the game, not that it had helped much. There were a bunch of younger girls who looked like sixth graders watching the game, probably there to cheer on someone's older brother. Oh well. Nothing was going to spoil her moment of triumph. Coach had come up with a brilliant routine as usual, and they were going to dazzle the halftime crowd.

Lili looked straight at the camera, hoping it captured her good side. "To be honest, I'm a little nervous."

"But aren't you used to performing?" the intern prodded.

"Yeah, but this is different."

Really, Lili wanted to dazzle one player in particular. The junior high match was already over, but the players were still around, most of them seated in the sidelines with their helmets off, resting and eating oranges. She'd already found Max on the far right corner of the field, wearing his red and black Reed Prep uniform. This little routine was All About Max, as far as Lili was concerned. She'd never been this sweet on a boy, unless you counted Zac Efron when she was in fifth grade.

She debated whether to reveal her crush on national television. Why not? Maybe it would garner her more votes. Surely a girl in love was always a sympathetic character.

"I'm nervous because a boy I really like is here," she said finally. She looked over her shoulder.

Max looked so incredibly darling today in his lacrosse uniform, with his giant padded gloves and crimson helmet, especially when he was pounding up and down the field. He'd scored two goals and four assists in the game. The Reed Prep Lions had beaten the crap out of the Gregory Hall Wolverines. And he could speak French! (Well, sort of.) He was amazing. She was glad to see he wasn't going anywhere.

Lili had arranged special dance-team outfits made for the occasion in Gregory Hall colors, blue and gold, designed by her cousin who used to work for Isaac Mizrahi. But the craziest thing about this performance was how easy it was to keep it from Ashley. Ashley was utterly preoccupied with having her own way on the banner and song and speeches for the Friendship Ceremony next week. And when she wasn't personally supervising the hand-stitching of every item, she was hanging out after school with loverboy Tri. With Ashley so busy, keeping the secret was easy—the hardest thing was finding time for rehearsals in Lili's own schedule.

"Let's go!" A.A. was jumping up and down in excitement, or maybe just to stay warm, since their outfits were a bit skimpy. Lauren looked a bit sick with nerves, especially when she noticed the size of the crowd. Lili knew extreme action was necessary. If Lauren was nervous, she'd make mistakes. And there was no way Lili was going to have the dance team made a laughing stock today. They were the Ashleys, after all, even if one of their usual members was AWOL.

"Lauren, you look fantastic. Doesn't she, A.A.?"

"Sure." A.A. leaned over to touch her toes. "Cute."

"Wow." Lauren gulped. "There are so many people. I didn't think anyone would actually be here. I hope I don't mess up."

"You won't—don't worry," Lili reassured her. "And even if one of us makes a tiny mistake, who cares? Just smile and they won't notice. This is all about fun!"

A.A. stared over at Lili as though she was out of her mind. Lili knew what she was thinking—last night she'd talked A.A.'s ear off about how stressed she was about the three of them messing up. Lili shrugged. Sometimes lies were necessary if you wanted to get a good performance out of someone. Seven years of violin recitals had taught her that.

"Right," Lauren said, doing a quick twirl and landing perfectly. "Okay, let's nail this thing!"

"Yeah, let's get out there," A.A. said quickly. "Coach is waving at us—he has the music ready."

The two Ashleys and Lauren walked slowly to the middle of the field. The thundering bass line of Missy Elliott's "Lose Control" blared from the overhead speakers.

"Everybody step, step," Lili called, and they all jumped to the left in perfect unison. The routine was going exactly as planned. A.A. was kicking so high she looked like a Rockette, and Lauren, to Lili's left, was keeping up without any problem. She even seemed to be enjoying herself. Lili hadn't been lying completely earlier—Lauren was gorgeous, and she looked hot in the slinky blue and gold minidress. She was the only girl at Miss Gamble's who could approach the poise and style of the Ashleys.

The best part of all was that Lili could sense they had the crowd's full attention. By the time they were thirty seconds into their routine, the boys in the stands were on their feet, hooting and clapping. Trent was glowing like a proud parent on the sidelines.

And with one final leaping kick, it was over.

Lili beamed up at the applauding crowd and the cameras, then sneaked a quick look down the sidelines. Where were the Reed Prep players? More to the point, where had Max gone? A few of them were huddled around, talking to their coach. If Max hadn't been watching, this whole performance was for nothing.

"Yay, Ashleys!" some of the sixth-grade girls in the stand were shrieking. "Yay, Lauren!"

Lauren waved up at them, looking as if she'd been used to adoring crowds all her life. Lili knew why the girls were all into Lauren now—no one had been admitted into the Ashleys' inner circle in a long time, and Lauren proved that maybe any of them could be an Ashley if they were lucky enough. If only the other girls knew they were only using Lauren to get on television.

"Come on," A.A. urged them, grabbing Lili's hand and motioning back toward the stands. "Game's about to start again."

It was true: The players were lining up, helmets already in place, most of them swinging their lacrosse nets. As the girls jogged back to where they'd left their things, one of the Gregory Hall players waved at them with his giant glove.

"Hey, Lauren!" Billy Reddy yelled through the grille in his helmet, looking like a fierce blue and gold tiger. "Thanks a lot!"

Next to her, Lili saw Lauren blush prettily.

But where was *her* guy? Had Max gone home?

"Hey, over there, someone's trying to get your attention," A.A. murmured in Lili's ear.

She looked over to where A.A. was pointing. Most of the

Reed Prep team were congregated to the side, but Lili didn't see Max anywhere . . . oh, wait. A.A. was right. There he was. Giving her a big thumbs-up sign.

"Great show!" he called.

"Good game, Max!" she yelled back, returning his smile. She checked to see if the camera had captured Max waving at her. Yes, it had. She beamed. All her planning had worked out just fine. She couldn't wait for French conversation class on Monday.

"Uh-oh." Lauren had picked up her bag and was staring up into the stands.

"What?" Lili followed her gaze. Maybe everything wasn't so perfect after all. Right in the back, hanging on to Tri's arm, was Ashley. And she looked p-i-s-s-e-d.

"I hope she's not angry with me for taking her place," said Lauren anxiously, though Lili thought a tad disingenuously. She seemed to still be reveling in the success of their performance.

"Don't worry." Lili squeezed Lauren's arm. "She's not mad at *you*."

"Why don't you guys go up there and say hi?" Jasper suggested, standing just outside of the shot.

Lili nodded. She'd known this was coming.

Ashley could be as mean as she liked, but she wouldn't care, Lili told herself. Ashley might think she had the

Preteen Queen title in the bag, but it was too late for her to take over the halftime show. Lili had outsmarted her.

But Lili didn't feel quite as brave as she would have liked as she climbed up the stadium steps to face the music.

ASHLEY PUTS ON HER GAME FACE

ASHLEY SLUMPED BACK IN HER SEAT AND tried to get interested in the lacrosse game. Or at least pretend to be interested. She was glad that Tri hadn't seen her face burn while the girls put on that shameless performance. He'd gotten up to get them drinks and popcorn at halftime, and when he returned, her so-called friends had already cleared the field.

Tri had played earlier, and Ashley had yelled her head off, not that it had done much good, since his team had been trounced badly. Like the rest of the guys, he was still wearing his uniform and had stayed to watch the high school team. Tri had been cool about losing, though, chalking it up to Reed Prep's better defense.

Ashley didn't think she could be as sporting. Especially since her dance team had practically been hijacked! What kind of team gave a performance without its captain? She was *boiling*.

Thank God she had a boyfriend. She didn't think she could face this humiliation alone. She gave Tri an affectionate arm squeeze, and he patted her knee absentmindedly. He was already in another world, on the edge of his seat, cheering on the Gregory Hall team, going crazy every time the boys in blue and gold got anywhere near the other team's net. At least this time their team was winning. The score was 5–4, apparently. Or was it? Ashley really wasn't paying attention.

She had a smile on her face, but inside was another story. Her best friends had planned and performed a dance routine for the television show without telling her. Without. Telling. Her. She would scream or kick something, but there was a camera planted in front of her face.

She wasn't sure what to do. This wasn't very Ashley at all. Usually the right plan of action came to her in a flash. This is what she did best. Hello.

And the best thing about the three Ashleys was exactly that—there were three of them. When A.A. wasn't around, she could assassinate her character with Lili. When Lili wasn't around, she and A.A. could buddy up and be the A-team. Three's a crowd, as the saying went, but to Ashley it was the perfect-size crowd. She could control it.

But now, with Lauren on the scene, a subtle power shift

was taking place. Lili had found an ally, someone who lent weight to her cause. There she was today, dancing in Lili's usual place. And where was Lili? Right in the center, in Ashley's preordained spot. So. Not. Cool. If Lili wanted to send a message to Ashley—that she was dispensable, and that someone else could take her place—then the message had been received, loud and clear.

Ashley did not need this. She had a lot on her mind right now. Tri *still* hadn't kissed her. He hadn't even *tried* to kiss her. After the cold reception she gave his good-bye hug, he'd started shaking her hand instead. What kind of a boyfriend just shook your hand? Maybe her beauty was intimidating. That's what her mother would say, if she told her. Not that she planned to share this particular nugget of information with anyone.

Unlike A.A., Ashley didn't want to be friends with a boy. She wanted a boyfriend—the kind who adored her and brought flowers and held her hand and kissed her. Tri was good-looking and adoring and sweet, but without the kiss he wasn't a real boyfriend. What was wrong with him? Surely there couldn't be something wrong with *her*?

"Ashley!" She heard A.A.'s voice and snapped to earth to see A.A., Lili, and Lauren all trooping up the stairs toward her, that idiot Jasper and several cameramen following.

She knew her friends probably felt guilty and were

coming over to make nice. Ashley had to think quickly. How was she going to behave? Frosty and furious? Sad and left out? So in love with Tri she didn't even notice their little performance?

She glanced at the camera and knew what she had to do.

"Hey, pretties!" she called gaily. "You guys rocked!"

"You're not mad?" Lili asked, squeezing in next to her and leaning in for the air kiss. Lauren plumped down at Lili's side, and A.A. quickly sidled in as well without meeting Ashley's eyes. At least one of them had the decency to look ashamed!

"What are you talking about? I'm so proud of all of you!" Ashley gushed.

Lili didn't even try to disguise her confusion, and Ashley was glad.

"Hey, A.A." Tri was leaning over Ashley to say hello. "We sucked today, huh?"

A.A. shrugged. "You guys got unlucky with a few of those calls."

"Yeah, well, our regular goalie has a sprained ankle. Hunter Mason. He just transferred here from Bellingham, and he's amazing. If he was playing, we would've won for sure." Tri grinned.

"I guess." A.A. said a bit dismissively. Ashley glanced at her friend. A.A. couldn't *still* be annoyed that Tri liked

Ashley more than her . . . what a crybaby! A.A. had had a million chances to hook up with Tri before—the two of them used to be irritatingly inseparable. It wasn't Ashley's fault if Tri preferred a more sophisticated girl.

"You're sure you're not mad?" Lili asked for what seemed like the hundredth time. It was almost as if Lili wanted a fight for the cameras. But Ashley wasn't about to give her one.

"Why would I be?" Ashley asked, as if it were the most ridiculous thing in the world.

"You know," Lili continued, smoothing down her blue and gold skirt. She was the only one of the three girls who hadn't changed after the routine. "If we'd had any idea you'd be here today, we would have insisted you take part in our little number. But you're impossible to track down. I guess you and Tri are just glued at the hip."

So this was the way they were going to play it. Ashley took a deep breath and considered for one brief, crazy moment the idea of letting Lili have it. There were so many things she could say right now about friendship and betrayal and lies and backstabbing . . . but no. The cameras. The votes. No one voted for a whiner. She had to let it go. Now was not the time to bitch-slap these ungrateful wenches who had forgotten that the Ashleys without Ashley was just a clique without a clue.

"I just have other things on my mind these days," she said

with a sigh, taking Tri's hand. Tri seemed kind of startled, but he flashed her a smile before focusing on the game again. "We have been spending *a lot* of time together."

She raised her eyebrows at Lili and gave a coy smile.

"I might," she said, lowering her voice to a whisper, "need to borrow some Chapstick." She winked at the camera. Hey, kissing your boyfriend didn't count as slutty.

"You bad girl," Lili murmured, giggling.

A.A. shifted uncomfortably in her seat. "I don't know why you guys are sitting all the way back here," she complained. "It's impossible to see a thing."

"Do you want to move forward?" asked Tri, swinging his head to gaze at A.A., but Ashley gripped his hand tightly. They weren't going anywhere, especially not if A.A. wanted it. The way he only joined the conversation when A.A. said something was annoying her.

"No point now," A.A. said sharply. She turned to Lauren to point something out about the opposing goalkeeper.

"So you're really not mad at us at all?" Lili probed, an edge of nervousness in her voice. That was the thing with Lili: She didn't have Ashley's nerve. If she wanted to brazen it out, she should stick with the plan. Really, she should listen and learn.

"Lil, will you chill out?" Ashley tinkled a silvery laugh. "As you say, I've been really busy this week. Learning a new routine just for a halftime show . . . well, there's not much point, is there?"

"I guess." Lili looked rattled now—yes! "Although if they win, this means they're going to the championships."

"That's nice." Ashley decided to play along with Lili's little delusion that she'd actually make a difference in the game's outcome. "And you guys really did look cute down there."

"Did you hear everyone applauding?" Lauren interrupted with a smile. Gag.

"They all thought it was fun, obviously. And so do I. Hey, if it's good for the Ashleys, it's good for me." Ashley checked her nails—she'd had them painted blue and gold that morning when Madame Kim and her team visited the house. Her mother was hosting a charity event tonight at the de Young, and Ashley had persuaded her to get a manicure and pedicure before the big event so she could get one too.

"Well, that's all we need," Jasper said from the side, looking disappointed. The guys turned the cameras off, and the production crew walked down the steps. Ashley was glad to see them go.

"Your nails look fab," said Lili. Back to fawning again. Just the way it should be.

"I wanted them to look special for tonight," Ashley told her. "I've got the goods on the hot postgame boy-girl party.

The first one of the school year." An idea began to form in her head. If Lili had organized a dance-team performance without her, what else had the little liar gotten on tape? Ashley would really have to ramp it up if she wanted to take the crown.

"Really?" A.A. was interested enough to take her eyes off the field.

"A party?" asked Lauren, who had probably never been invited to a party in her life, let alone a real boy-girl one.

"That's right. It was supposed to be the Gregory Hall victory party, but now it's more like a consolation thing since they lost."

They all looked excited at the invitation, even sulky A.A., and Ashley was satisfied. She'd made the right decision taking the high road and not acting all pissy. Stop the presses: Ashley had saved the day, as usual!

She slid out her cell phone and discreetly sent a message to Jasper's number. If he wanted conflict, action, and dramatic tension, she knew just the thing that would deliver.

BE! AGGRESSIVE! B-E AGGRESSIVE! B-E, A-GEE-GEE, ARR-EEE-ESS, ESS-EYE-VEE, EEE! What's your favorite cheer? Ours is the one that the cheerleaders can never spell quite right. Somewhere along the double g's and the double s's, their tongues get tied. Not that there were any cheering bee mishaps during the splendid performance by the Ashleys dance team at last weekend's lacrosse match!

#1 ASHLEY SPENCER

STYLE: 9

She sat out the performance but managed to look so poised in the stands we've got to give her this week anyway. But points off for the tacky blue and gold nails.

SOCIAL PRESENCE: 10

The best way to support Gregory Hall is to date one of its hot students!

SMILE: 10

We also love how supportive she was of her friends!

SMARTS: 10

Probably a good idea to skip the performance. She doesn't need all that extra attention!

CUMULATIVE SCORE: 39

#2 ASHLEY "A.A." ALIOTO

STYLE: 10

Who can watch a couple of guys chase a ball
around with a stick when A.A. is doing pirouettes?

SOCIAL PRESENCE: 10

Didn't blink even when the Gregory Hall mascot
practically mauled her after the dance.

SMILE: 8

Only because hers disappeared once the routine
was over.

SMARTS: 9

Probably the only girl there who actually knows
how the game is played.

CUMULATIVE SCORE: 37

next >>

#2 (TIE) ASHLEY "LILI" LI

STYLE: 10

Looks great in blue and gold, but maybe her true colors are red and black?

SOCIAL PRESENCE: 10

We loved seeing Miss Lili in the center for once!

SMILE: 10

Is it just us or is something sizzling in the air between the organization queen and the Reed Prep lax king?

SMARTS: 7

Is it wise to root for the opposing team?

CUMULATIVE SCORE: 37

#6 LAUREN PAGE

STYLE: 9

Unlike Sheridan Riley, this one can pass as an
Ashley any day.

SOCIAL PRESENCE: 9

Her dance-team debut went off without a hitch!

SMILE: 7

Finally beginning to surface!

SMARTS: 8

The only dancer who thought to wear nude tights
with the skimpy costume to fend off frostbite!

CUMULATIVE SCORE: 33

11

THE LYING AND THE SWITCH
INSIDE THE WARDROBE

A.A. HAD BEEN TO BOY-GIRL PARTIES before. Ashley hadn't exaggerated, though, when she described this party as hot. First of all, the place was amazing. It was way cooler than a house: It was a three-level loft apartment in trendy downtown SoMa. The building used to be a warehouse, so the ceilings were sky-high, the walls were exposed brick, and a curling wrought-iron staircase linked each floor with the next. The apartment belonged to one of the Gregory Hall players, whose parents were on a six-week cruise on the Aegean Sea and who left the apartment and their son in the care of their practically deaf, genial butler, who was safely ensconced in his room, watching BBC America.

She loved the industrial-style kitchen on the first floor,

which led into a vast sunken living room. The kitchen counter was covered with dozens of empty and half-empty soda and energy-drink cans and open bags of chips and pretzels. The only furniture in the living room was an oversize, low-slung, L-shaped couch, one side of which was as wide as a twin-size bed. The entire length of the back wall was covered with bookshelves. If she was going to have a city pad when she grew up, this was what it would look like.

Someday she hoped to live in a house by the ocean in Malibu, but this would be a perfect place to flop whenever she came home to see her family and do some shopping. The living room opened up to a multilevel terrace with a view of the entire city, the Transamerica building a bright pyramid in the sky. A.A. wandered around, taking everything in. There were a ton of kids at the party, but most of the boys seemed to have segregated onto the lower floors, playing poker, darts, or ping-pong, while the girls were huddled in groups by the staircase, talking about the boys.

She waved hello to the other Miss Gamble's girls, surprised that so many had been invited. Usually only the Ashleys and their SOAs were at events like this, but it looked like word had trickled down to everybody. Was that really Guinevere "Lollipop Head" Parker by the stereo? A.A. was also a bit surprised to notice that a crew of sixth graders had been able to crash the party as well.

There was an intense game of Truth or Dare going down in the back room, and A.A. steered clear of that scene. She liked kissing boys—sort of. That is, she'd like to kiss a boy she liked, if that made sense. For one blissful month this summer, she'd been looking forward to meeting (and kissing) laxjock, her online sweetheart.

But he'd turned out to be a mirage. Or possibly—probably—Tri. If only she'd been able to talk to him about it, but she never had a chance. Ever since the dance, Tri was all over Ashley like a rash. The real reason A.A. was constantly on the move, climbing over people to get up the stairs, dawdling out on the terrace and wandering into rooms where she didn't know anyone, was this: She wanted to avoid Ashley and Tri.

The sight of those two lovebirds turned her stomach. A.A. leaned over the edge of the third-floor terrace, gazing out at the lights of the city. Despite her outbursts of evil, Ashley had her moments, and she was one of A.A.'s best friends. And so was Tri. She should be happy they liked each other and wanted to spend time together. Right? Wrong.

Sometimes A.A. wished they'd never met. What was up with her? Sure, she missed Tri—the two of them used to spend hours just hanging out, playing video games, or just . . . doing a lot of nothing. That was it, right? She was just a little jealous that he didn't have as much time to hang out with her as before. So why did Ashley's comment about needing so much Chap Stick gross her out? One thing she knew for sure—she certainly didn't want to witness the two of them play tonsil hockey all night.

"You must be A.A." A tall guy with his foot in a brace hobbled over to stand near her, resting his back against the steel railings and swigging from a plastic cup. "Tri told me all about you. I'm Hunter Mason."

"Hey." Ashley mustered a smile. So this was the phenomenal goalie Tri had told her about. But what did he mean, Tri had told him all about her? What was there to tell? Mean stories about making out with Saint A's boys, probably. Or maybe about how he'd posed as laxjock and led her on for a month before standing her up. She was probably the butt of every joke at Gregory Hall. "What did Tri say exactly? That I beat him in every video game he owns?"

"Pretty much, and that you were a cool chick." Hunter smiled.

A.A. relaxed a little. Okay, so maybe Tri wasn't bad-mouthing her. And maybe Hunter wasn't a sleazy guy trying to hit on an easy target. He was tall for his age—unlike Tri—and if his hair hadn't been bright orange, he'd be pretty good-looking. They chatted together for a while, and she found out that Hunter was an only child, and like her, lived with his divorced mom.

When it started to get windy and wet out on the terrace,

they stepped into the high-tech office, A.A. sitting on the metal-gray Aeron office chair and Hunter perching on the edge of the desk. But just as she was starting to relax, out of the corner of her eye A.A. spotted Ashley out in the hallway. She had Tri by the hand, as if she couldn't bear to be parted from him for even one second. Ashley was even wearing a sweatshirt that had "Ashley and Ti" embroidered on it. Ugh.

She could hear Ashley telling someone they wanted to look at the telescope in the office. A.A. froze. They'd probably come in, see A.A. and Hunter, and then all four of them would soon be hanging out, like some kind of instant double date. A.A. felt her chest constrict. She had to get away. But where?

The rain was heavy now, and the terrace was uncovered. No escape there. But if she walked out of the room, she'd bump smack into Tri and Ashley. There was no place to hide, except for a storage closet in the corner. A.A. watched, fascinated, as the closet door suddenly opened and a boy and a girl stumbled out of it, giggling. She'd heard a bunch of people were playing some game called Seven Minutes in Heaven, where you had to spend seven minutes with a boy in a closet. The whole point of the game was to kiss each other. But when the seven minutes was over, so was your relationship.

She heard footsteps outside the door. Tri and Ashley,

her so-called best friends, would be there at any second. She had to hide.

Hunter must have noticed the desperate, urgent way she was looking at the closet door, because he suddenly spoke up. "Hey, you wanna play?" he asked, touching her sleeve. "Seven minutes?" he teased.

"Um . . ." A.A. stalled. Hunter seemed like a nice enough guy, but there was no way *that* was going to happen. She wasn't about to make out with him. She'd only met him ten minutes ago. But before she could say anything, Hunter was across the room in a flash, opening the closet door and stepping in and beckoning her with a raise of his eyebrow.

A.A. took a deep breath and followed him. Ashley's voice was getting louder and closer, with Tri right behind her. There wasn't a moment to lose. She had to get out of the room and away from them. But if Hunter thought she was going to kiss him, he had another thought coming.

Three strides and she was across the room. She stepped into the closet, tripping on a box of copy paper while a coat hanger knocked against the side of her head. Hunter was pulling the door closed, but before he could close it all the way, A.A. put a hand on his arm.

"Look, it's a long story, but I just need a place to hang out for a few minutes. There's someone I don't particularly want to see right now. And I don't want to play that game or whatever. Is that cool?"

To her surprise, Hunter looked more relieved than anything else.

"'Course it's cool," he said, nodding.

She was so thankful she gave him a friendly hug as she reached back to clutch the door handle. But if she thought she'd escaped an awkward scene, she was wrong.

Because the last thing she saw before she closed the door was Tri's face, surprised and disapproving, staring straight into her eyes.

LAUREN'S NEW MANTRA? SAVE THE LACROSSE PLAYERS. SAVE THE WORLD.

AUREN WOUND HER WAY UP THE STAIRS TO THE second floor of the loft apartment, stepping over the gossiping girls hanging over the banisters, trying to keep Lili in her sights. Lauren was used to lofts— her own bedroom in the huge new mansion her parents had bought at the Marina had a sleep-and-play second floor—but she *definitely* wasn't used to boy-girl parties.

Dex had gone a little overboard in preparing her for the event. He told her to make sure she poured her own drinks, preferably from a sealed bottle or unopened can, so she could be sure nobody had added anything weird before she got to it. She didn't think any of the boys would try anything like that, since most of them didn't even try to talk to a girl, let alone take advantage of one. But Dex was Dex.

Overprotective. Still, maybe he had a point. Lauren cracked the seal on a liter bottle of Sprite and poured it into a clean cup. So far so good.

"And whatever you do," Dex had told her, "don't get dragged into any activity that involves kissing in closets for seven minutes. If a boy really likes you, he'll ask you out. You're a really pretty girl, Lauren. You don't need to make out with a stranger in the dark to get a boyfriend."

Dex had never said anything so blush-inducing to Lauren before. Most of the time all they did was tease each other and call each other "ugly."

She noticed that Lili was moving quickly through the crowd, climbing the next flight of stairs to the loft's top floor. By the time Lauren squeezed past a burly guy trying to balance a lampshade on his head, she had disappeared. Music pumped on every floor of the loft, and each room was crowded with good-looking kids hanging out. She tightened her grip on her plastic cup of Sprite, trying not to spill anything as she made awkward progress up the winding stairs. The last thing she wanted to do was draw attention to herself.

Part of her wanted to sit in a corner sipping her drink and simply watch everyone else have a good time. But that was the old Lauren, she chided herself, the one with frizzy hair, baby fat, and bad clothes. The new Lauren was a star on a reality show, had her hair cut by Christophe twice a month in Beverly Hills, and had her clothes bought with the help of an army of personal shoppers.

So this was what being one of the Ashleys was all about—high kicks at the lacrosse game and now high jinks at a boy-girl party. Last year all she did was watch *Heroes* reruns on Friday nights, crushing on the cute one who could absorb other people's power.

If she could just absorb enough of the Ashleys' popularity to become popular herself, then maybe she could make a difference. So far, they seemed to be content with letting her be part of the group as long as the television cameras were on, but what would happen when the show was over?

Lauren looked around. She was glad to see a bunch of girls from class looking thrilled to be there as well. She'd casually mentioned the party in an e-mail to Guinevere Parker, suggesting it might be a good event to cover for her "Page Seven" social column in the school paper and adding that anyone and everyone from the seventh-grade class would be welcome to attend.

Lauren decided to climb the final flight of stairs and look for Lili and the rest of the Ashleys. Pay dirt! The bathroom door was open and there was Lili, sitting on the marble countertop, legs swinging, chatting with three other girls and comparing lip glosses.

Lauren waved, and Lili fluttered her fingers in acknowledgment. Lauren hesitated, wondering if she should join her, but there wasn't any more space on the counter. She moved on.

In the giant home office, with sleek gray furniture, a flat-screen thirty-inch G5 computer, and a dinosaur-size telescope, she found Ashley and Tri in the corner talking to some other kids. A.A. always went on about how short Tri was, but that didn't take away from the fact that he was by far the handsomest guy in the Gregory Hall seventh grade. He was so good-looking he could be an actor—weren't they all short too?

Lauren ambled up to them just as Ashley stood up from the couch and pulled Tri to standing.

"You're leaving?" Lauren asked.

"Just to get some fresh air," said Ashley. "It's finally stopped raining."

"Have you seen A.A.?" Lauren hadn't seen her since they'd arrived at the party.

"Nope." Ashley shook her head.

She felt shy about joining Ashley and Tri and drifted to another room. Lauren looked at her now-empty cup. Her bravado faded a little. She was at a party, but the Ashleys had deserted her once again. Maybe if she walked down to the kitchen for a refill, that would kill a little more time until

Dex had to pick her up. She noticed an overweight guy who looked more like he was in college than high school standing alone in a corner, but he seemed kind of strange and not very friendly. He was staring into space, a backpack hanging off one of his shoulders.

"Oh crap." A guy came over to stand next to her. His face was flushed. He had a mess of dark blond hair and twinkling green eyes, and had a huge dark stain in the middle of his rugby shirt.

"Nice move, huh?" he asked, rubbing at it. "I wasn't even playing and I get sloshed." He shook his head. "I guess it goes with this one," he added, pointing to a red ketchup stain.

Lauren smiled and handed him a few napkins. She recognized him as one of the guys who hung with Tri Fitzpatrick. It was kind of cute how he cared about his shirt. Most guys were totally comfortable running around in rags.

"How bad does it look?" he asked.

She shrugged. "It looks okay. You can't even see it."

"Good." He heaved a dramatic sigh. "Some Miss Gamble's girls would make me leave the room or tell me to go home and change."

Lauren couldn't help looking over at Ashley, standing outside on the terrace, talking to Tri, not a hair out of place. Ashley would probably think that a soda stain was an insult and a ketchup stain was an abomination.

"As long as it's not blood," Lauren cautioned.

"I swear it isn't. Unless a Reed Prep defender stabbed me on the way up the stairs, Crashers," he said with a smile, motioning to a group of loud boys who had just arrived.

Lauren followed his gaze, and sure enough, there were a bunch of guys from the Reed Prep team making their way into the loft. The Gregory Hall guys didn't seem too fazed by the appearance of their rivals. Most of them were friends who'd gone to the same preschools.

"Then you'll live, I guess," she said with a laugh.

"I guess." He sighed. "If you say so."

Could this be happening? Was Lauren Page actually flirting with a guy? And was he actually flirting back?

By the time his friends dragged him away—they were hitting some other party in St. Francis Wood—Christian had asked for her phone number.

As soon as he left, Lauren ended up talking to another boy who'd wandered over looking for something to wipe up a spill on the coffee table. She happily supplied him with several napkins as well. Like Christian, he was a lax player, but he was in seventh grade at St. A's. It seemed it was her duty to save the boys from dirt that night.

He was easy on the eyes as well, but in a different way from Christian. Alex was dark, with olive skin and eyes that looked almost black. She helped him mop up the mess, and they fell into a deep conversation, taking about everything from the music at the party to the freakishly bad weather they were having in San Francisco.

She told him about her parents, and he told her about his family. His grandmother was Catalan, he said, and she used to sing to him in Spanish when he was a little boy. When he got all embarrassed and apologized, saying he didn't usually talk about his personal life, Lauren's heart melted like a gelato on a hot day. Something about Alex's dark, brooding eyes and the way his hair flopped over his face made her feel squishy and silly. When he asked for her number, she gave it to him without hesitation.

Lauren looked around the room. There was still no sign of the Ashleys anywhere, but she didn't mind. Two boys had asked for her number, and neither of them had tried to drag her into a closet.

Boys liking her. How weird was that? Nothing like this had ever happened to her before. But then again, that was LBTA. Life Before the Ashleys.

13

THEY SAY A KISS CAN BE A COMMA, A QUESTION MARK, OR AN EXCLAMATION POINT, BUT FOR LILI IT'S ALL THREE

LILI SPOTTED MAX AS SOON AS HE ARRIVED AT THE party, and she knew he'd seen her, too. Their eyes met from across the room (really from above the room, since she was gazing down at the first floor from the second). He gave her a shy smile and her heart flip-flopped, but she tried not to show it, focusing on the makeup advice one of the eighth graders was dishing.

She had to play it cool and not act as though she was a desperate sports groupie with a massive crush on a lax star.

Even though that's exactly what she was.

Lili gave herself one hour to float around the party, check out the entire loft, air kiss everyone she knew, and flirt with as many random boys as possible. One hour to let Max see her walking up and down the curving iron staircase wearing her cute dress with the super-short hem and her new tango shoes with the three-inch heels. One hour for him to notice her glossy hair swinging and her pink lips smiling. After the hour was over, she would make sure she got as close to him as possible and stayed there.

Like all of Lili's plans, this one worked like a charm.

After sashaying the length and breadth of the loft numerous times, she found herself in the middle of a crush of people standing in the hallway. They were all waiting to get onto the terrace, where someone was supposed to shoot fireworks. She wormed her way through until she was near-but-not-too-near him, hoping it would look natural that she was just by his elbow.

Max turned around and looked pleasantly surprised. "Hey!"

"Hey, you," she said lightly, as if she had just noticed he was standing there. "What are you doing here? Aren't you guys, like, the enemy?"

"We were invited!" Max protested. "What's a victory party without the real victors?" he joked.

Lili smiled. A few people behind her jostled her to the front, pressing her closer to him. "Oops. Sorry!"

Max steadied her and returned her smile. Lili thought the two of them must look a little funny, just standing there smiling at each other, but she felt really happy. She was sure she was getting a vibe off him. He liked her, too.

"Madame LeBrun's a real trip, isn't she?" asked Lili.

"I think I counted fifty-five sneezes last session." Max laughed. "Is she allergic to everything?"

Lili nodded eagerly. "That's nothing. Last year it got so bad she fainted!"

"Really?"

"You should have seen it. She was sneezing so much, and then she kind of swooned and tripped over the rug and hit her head on the floor. She was bleeding so badly, me and Greg—the other guy who used to be in the class—thought we'd have to call 911."

"No way!"

"Yeah. It didn't happen. I made it up." She winked. What had gotten into her?

Max looked confused for a second, and then he laughed. His shoulders relaxed, and he grinned down at her. "You're a real trip too." He moved closer to her to make room for a couple of people who'd squeezed past them to get to the terrace. Outside, they could hear the first whiz-bangs of the bottle rockets. More people crowded into the hallway in an attempt to get out to the terrace, and the next explosions were so loud Lili had to hold her hands to her ears.

"Wanna duck in here?" Max asked, finding a door that led to a small butler's pantry. "Just until it's all clear?"

Lili nodded, glad to be away from the mob and the noise. The pantry was a small, dark space. They stood so close to each other that his denim-clad knee was almost touching her bare one.

"So Madame didn't faint. How can I trust you now?" asked Max, arching an eyebrow in the dim light.

"Are you calling me a liar, Maxwell Costa?" she demanded, pretending to be completely indignant.

"Your words, not mine, Ashley Li."

It was the first time he'd said her name. And he called her Ashley, which no one ever did, which made it sound more intimate, more special. Then the two of them were standing so close together she was practically in his arms, and his head was bent down very close to hers. Someone's elbow—hers? his?—brushed the light switch, and then it was so dark she could barely make out his face. Neither of them spoke, and Lili knew what was about to happen.

He was going to kiss her.

She closed her eyes and their lips met.

Whatever the Ashleys believed, Lili *had* kissed a boy before. But it wasn't anything like this. Just like she told her friends, she'd kissed a boy in Taiwan last summer. The boy was a friend of Lili's cousin, a thirteen-year-old who was cute, shy, and nervous. That was the problem. He was so shy and nervous that when he went to kiss her, he actually missed her mouth and kissed her on the chin! It was pretty icky. Wet and cold and unexpected, totally disappointing, and the boy was so embarrassed he never came anywhere near her again.

Her friends didn't have to know *all* the gory details, and there was no way they'd ever find out. Unless Ashley was planning to send spies to Taiwan to track down the truth, of course. Lili wouldn't put anything past her.

But this kiss was completely different. This kiss was soft but confident, utterly intense. Her mouth went dry, and she could barely remember how to speak English, let alone French.

She lost herself in his kiss, and all the stress in her life— the competition with Ashley for the Preteen Queen crown, the parental pressure to succeed academically, the constant surveillance and assessment on AshleyRank—floated away. She soared ten feet into the air.

When they finally pulled away from each other, Max drummed his fingers on the wall and looked away. When he turned back to her, an alarm rang in Lili's head. Something was up. His cute face was troubled, as though he'd just remembered something really bad.

"Is everything okay?" she managed to say, still breathless from the kiss.

"Yeah, yeah." He couldn't even look her in the eyes. "It's just . . . weird."

"What's weird?" Now she was nervous. Now she was *terrified*.

"I mean, uh, I'll see you around, okay?"

See you around?

Uh-oh. Lili didn't like the sound of that.

"Look, I'll call you. . . ." Max let her hand go and opened the door.

"Where are you going?" she asked. "Can't we talk about this?" What was going on? Why was he acting so freaked out? It was just a kiss. Did she have cooties or something? Why was he acting like he wanted nothing more than to be really, really far away from her? Was this what happened when you kissed a bad boy? Was her mom right?

"Bye," Max said, moving so fast that he knocked into some fat guy with a backpack.

Then, just like that, he walked away, leaving Lili to walk out alone into the now deserted hallway, her face crumbling into tears.

Our hearts are still pounding from all the Red Bull we drank at the first B-G (that's Boy-Girl) party of the year! Whoohoo!

#1 ASHLEY SPENCER

STYLE: 10

We heart that Boy Meets Girl Deesh sweatshirt she was wearing, which had Adorable Boyfriend's name on top of a silhouette of a little boy and her name above a silhouette of a little girl. Way to wear your heart on your sleeve!

SOCIAL PRESENCE: 10

Because she's one-half of the seventh grade's It Couple.

SMILE: 10

Bestowed upon one and all.

SMARTS: 9

Took a pass on the chip selection. Probably a good idea. (Burp!)

CUMULATIVE SCORE: 39

#2 ASHLEY "A.A." ALIOTO

STYLE: 10

Always looks effortlessly chic. Bet her cool
asymmetrical top was yet another hand-me-down
from her model mom.

SOCIAL PRESENCE: 9

Disappearing into a closet with a new boy? If she
doesn't watch out, she'll start to get a reputation!

SMILE: 8

The Closet Queen didn't look too happy once
the doors opened.

SMARTS: 8

Not sure it's wise to get another boy all hot and
bothered about you when you just got rid of
your former stalker!

CUMULATIVE SCORE: 35

next >>

#2 ASHLEY "LILI" LI

STYLE: 10

Looked so girly-pretty in a breezy, romantic, dove gray minidress accented with a floppy bow.

SOCIAL PRESENCE: 10

Smooth operator, dazzled all the boys at the party, including one particular Reed Prep player.

SMILE: 8

Never seen her looking more joyful at the beginning, but she left party looking upset. Does anyone know what happened??

SMARTS: 7

Skirt looked a little short for constant up-and-down on the stairs.

CUMULATIVE SCORE: 35

#6 LAUREN PAGE

STYLE: 10

Her silk jersey Foley & Corrina dress (we asked!)

was just too cute!

SOCIAL PRESENCE: 8

Spotted flirting with not one but two boys at the bash!

But maybe that's too much of a good thing?

SMILE: 7

Practically a little Miss Sunshine these days.

SMARTS: 9

Word has it she was behind our invitation.

Nice move!

CUMULATIVE SCORE: 34

THE ONLY THING ASHLEY IS
CELEBRATING IS HERSELF

THE FRIENDSHIP CEREMONY WAS GENIUS—
even if Ashley had to say so herself. She'd come up
with it on the spot in that producers' meeting and
now, just a week later, it was a reality. Not just that: It was
reality television. How cool was that?

In front of the cameras in Miss Charm's class, groups of
nervous girls stood up to make their presentations. Ashley
wasn't surprised they were nervous. She'd be nervous as well
if the Ashleys had made such pathetic banners.

Just as she predicted, everyone went for the most obvious
thing. Sheridan Riley had stuck a row of false eyelashes onto
her group's banner to represent her (too short) bangs.
Melody Myers and Olivia DeBartolo had stuck Olsen Twin
paper dolls onto their banner to show how similar and

inseparable they were. Gag. Some people had actually used *colored pens* to make their banners. Hello! Were they poor? Or just lazy? Ashley couldn't believe the lack of initiative.

Even the songs everyone else chose were totally pre-dictable. The first group sang "You've Got a Friend," which was some kind of hippie song that Ashley's father sometimes played on his guitar. It was super sappy, and not helped by the fact that two of the four girls were crying while they were singing. The second group was even more lame, singing the old Beatles song "A Little Help from My Friends." Daria Hart actually looked like Ringo. Ashley had to pinch herself so she wouldn't explode in hysterics.

But she had to admit that Daria's group—the three mousiest girls in the class—hadn't done a bad job with their banner. They'd used the cover from the Beatles album *Sgt. Pepper's Lonely Hearts Club Band*, because that was where their song was from, and they'd had their three plain-Jane faces photo-shopped in. At least they'd made an effort. Miss Charm was oohing and aahing over it, but she hadn't seen the Ashleys' banner yet.

Melody and Olivia's group tried to sing the theme song from *Sex and the City*, but since there were no words, they got a little confused around the "bum, ba bum" parts. In their speech, they talked about one another as though they were all characters from the show. "You're so like Carrie," Melody

127

said to Doro Hansen. "Flaky, goofy, but with really pretty hair." The problem was that even though there were four of them, no one wanted to be Samantha, the slutty one, so there were two Charlottes instead.

The Ashleys—and Lauren—were up last, just as the producer had requested. Their 3-D banner looked amazing. Even Lili, who'd turned into an attention hogger and whiny baby ever since the cameras showed up, had let Ashley use her superior designs, realizing that Ashley actually knew what she was talking about.

Lili had been acting a little weird all day. She'd left the party last Saturday red-eyed, without telling anyone what happened. Ashley heard something had happened with the Reed Prep Froggy (because he was taking French, geddit) and vowed to get to the bottom of that, and she hoped whatever it was wouldn't affect Lili's participation in the program.

Everyone in the room gasped when they unfurled the heavy, ivory-colored canvas, Lauren holding one end and A.A. holding the other. Ashley was represented, as planned, by a giant diamanté tiara sewn onto the canvas. To shut Lili up, they'd mocked up a Blackberry, just as she requested, getting an oversize replica made from hand-stitched black leather. For A.A. they cut a soccer ball in half and glued one side to the banner. Ashley had never been serious about the kissing thing—she was just saying all that for the camera to create a sensation.

The trouble with A.A.: She was gorgeous. With her sharp cheekbones and long legs, she looked like a model. Plus she had a naturally sweet personality, and Ashley couldn't have A.A. coming across on TV like the angelic, beautiful one. The public had a right to know she could be a bit of a ho.

A.A. had forgiven Ashley for her jibes, as Ashley knew she would. Well, she'd let the matter drop, which was almost the same thing. With Lili being so pouty and difficult all of a sudden, and Tri still acting like a pretend boyfriend, still not brave enough to kiss her, Ashley didn't need any more stress on her hands.

The hardest person to represent on the banner was Lauren, for obvious reasons. They didn't really know her, and it was hard to tell what her personality was, exactly. She did well at school and her parents were insanely rich. So what? Everyone who was anyone at Miss Gamble's was rich. Finally they decided on a mock-up menu from the Ivy, the restaurant they'd gone to in L.A., to represent how she knew a lot of cool places. Ashley got the calligrapher her mother used for black-tie events to reproduce the menu exactly by hand.

Across the center of the banner, the words "The Ashleys" had been hand-embroidered by one of her maids, who came from Guatemala. And each of them had a speech to make (learned by heart, of course, and rehearsed ad infinitum) about one of the other group members. Lili did Lauren, as she was the only one who wanted to. Lauren did Ashley, and she had lots of nice things to say. It was so obvious that Lauren was behind the blog. She seemed to hero-worship Ashley. *But then*, Ashley thought, *who didn't?* A.A. did Lili, and she did a decent job of praising Lili's loyalty, and Ashley finished off with a heartfelt speech about A.A. This was a celebration of friendship, after all. And looking around at her group, Ashley felt a wellspring of sincere affection for them. They made her look so good.

Their song was the pièce de résistance, as Lili insisted on calling it. They decided to take a completely different approach from all the other groups and *not* choose a song with the word "friends" in it. So they finally decided on "Beautiful" by Christina Aguilera. "We are beautiful in every single way" seemed like the perfect way to describe how they felt about one another. Plus it totally showcased Ashley's sweet singing voice. She was so glad she'd insisted on everyone singing a capella. If musical accompaniment were allowed, Lili would have brought in her violin and stolen the limelight.

After class ended, and the producers were packing up and everyone was gushing over one another's banners and performances, Jasper—the British one, who was cuter than Matt, Ashley decided, mainly because of his accent—gave Ashley a cheeky grin.

"You may just have this sewn up," he said, clapping her on the shoulder. "If you keep this up, you'll be the one everyone votes for. And by the way, thanks for the tip the other night."

"My pleasure." Ashley smiled.

"What did Jasper say to you?" asked Lili keenly.

"Nothing important." Ashley shrugged. She didn't want to give Lili any more incentive to stage another secret taping.

Subterfuge was the only way to win. No one had ever won a game show by being nice.

LAUREN SAYS IF YOU CAN'T BE WITH THE ONE YOU LOVE, LOVE THE ONE YOU'RE WITH

AUREN HAD A DATE. HER FIRST DATE! TWO FIRST dates, actually. On the same day, and in pretty much the same place. How did this happen?

First off, Christian called to ask if she wanted to go hang out in Golden Gate Park one day after school. He sounded kind of nervous and almost apologetic about it: He was working on an urban geography project for school and needed to do some research at the Japanese Tea Garden. At the party, Lauren had said that the park was one of her favorite places in the city. Would she like to come along?

Of course she would! Lauren used to go to Golden Gate Park all the time when she was a little girl, because her parents didn't have much money and the park was free. Her father had been a graduate teaching assistant for most of her childhood, working on his PhD and scraping by on an academic stipend, while her mother had a part-time job at a not-for-profit organization that paid her almost nothing to answer the phone and type letters. Their favorite place to spend time on Sunday afternoons was the Japanese Tea Garden. Of course, she hadn't mentioned all that stuff about being poor to Christian. He was a Gregory Hall boy, and not a scholarship student. She didn't want him to know that she used to live in a walk-up in the Mission.

Over the weekend, Alex had called as well. His mother was hosting some big, boring cocktail reception—"the usual socialite shindig," he told her on the phone, "comb-overs and canapés"—at the de Young museum in the park. The museum closed at five, but the reception didn't begin until six. Did Lauren want to hang out there for an hour?

With all the crowds gone, they could have their own private tour of the place. He remembered her saying at the party how much she liked the park and the museum. *Oh God,* Lauren thought, *I must have gone around saying the same things to everyone! I really need to work on my conversation skills.*

Of course, the night of Alex's museum event had to be Wednesday, the one afternoon Christian could meet her in the Japanese Tea Garden. Lauren took a deep breath and agreed to do both. What had she done? Was she hanging out with the Ashleys so much that she was turning into one of them?

Going out with two boys at the same time was just the sort of duplicitous, selfish thing an Ashley would do. But Lauren couldn't help it! She liked both of them—what was wrong with that? It wasn't like they were exclusive or anything. She was just having fun.

Besides, an Ashley would most definitely *not* go to the Japanese Tea Garden. The other day, when she was having lunch with the Ashleys, Lili had dissed the fortune cookie that they were giving out on International Day, saying that they were actually an American invention. Just like sweet and sour pork and General Tso's chicken. Then Lauren piped up and told them how, a hundred years ago, fortune cookies were invented by the Japanese gardener who looked after the Tea Garden in the park.

She'd thought the girls were interested, so she had kept talking—about how someone in L.A. claimed to have invented them, and how the Court of Historical Review had finally decided that they originated in San Francisco—until Ashley finally held up a hand to stop her and said it was the most boring story she'd ever heard.

Luckily, Christian didn't seem to find it boring. She told him all about it as they crossed one of the stepping-stone paths and circled a beautiful, serene lily pond. He was still in his Gregory Hall uniform, his shirt hanging out and his dark blond hair so messy it looked like he'd done somersaults down a hill to get here.

Lauren had raced home after school to change, telling Dex to drive as fast as possible. He ignored her, of course, and drove at his usual speed, laughing at her for trying to cram too many dates into one afternoon. She decided on jeans and a casual T-shirt with a funny slogan, "Don't Waste My Daytime Minutes," that she hoped would appeal to Christian's sense of humor.

Somehow she felt less pressure hanging out with a boy like Christian than with the Ashleys. Or with any of the girls at Miss Gamble's, actually. He didn't even seem to care what she was wearing, aside from cracking up at her T-shirt. He just smiled at her a lot and tried to make her laugh by pretending to almost fall off one of the stepping-stones.

Lauren especially loved the steep, curving moon bridge, which was more like a ladder than a bridge you walked over. She used to love clambering up it when she was a little girl, using her hands to pull herself up to the top.

"It's modeled on an ancient Chinese canal crossing," Lauren explained to Christian, and he very seriously wrote that down in his notebook. She'd been worried he'd think she was too geeky, but he didn't seem to mind.

"Race you to the top?" he suggested, nodding toward the

bridge, and she started running right away—without a head start, she'd never beat him!

They were having such a good time that when she pulled out her phone to check the time, Lauren was startled. With a pang, she realized it was almost five and time to meet Alex. She was reluctant to leave him.

"I've got to meet my mom now," she said. She hated having to lie to Christian, but it seemed kind of rude to tell him she was off on a date with another boy. "For this reception thing at the museum I told you about—I'm really sorry I have to go."

She *was* sorry. Hanging out with Christian was a lot of fun. She really liked him a lot.

"That's okay," he said. "Hey, you wanna go see that new disaster movie next week? The one with the robots taking over the world or something?"

"Don't the robots always take over the world?" asked Lauren.

"But of course! Me, I'm scared of my iPod, aren't you?" Christian laughed.

"Oh, completely, and I'm not too sure about this cell phone either." She grinned. "It's either going to give me cancer or take control of my brain."

"I'll text you," he promised.

She had another date with Christian! Whee. But first she had to get through date number two.

Christian gave her a quick hug, and when he was gone, Lauren ran all the way to the de Young museum, pounding through the elegant sculpture garden and arriving at the main entrance of the distinctive, copper-covered building pretty much out of breath. She hoped Alex wouldn't notice too much.

In a nearby restroom, she changed into outfit number two: a short, strapless, satin Rhys Dwfen dress with sky-high Alexandra Neel slingbacks.

Alex was waiting for her outside. Dark-haired, smoldering Alex, whose face broke into a giant smile when he saw her. The butterflies in her stomach returned.

"Sorry I'm late," she wheezed, desperately trying to straighten her dress collar and flatten her flyaway hair as they walked through the first courtyard.

Inside the sweeping central court of the museum, with its high ceilings, pale stone floor, and giant black-and-white photographic mural, caterers were setting up food stations and bars. A tall, dark-haired woman in a silk Lanvin dress, her hair in a chic bun, was talking to waiters in tuxedoes.

"That's my mother," whispered Alex, grabbing Lauren's arm. "Unless you want to be put to work filling ice buckets, we better get outta here."

They ducked into one of the adjoining galleries, which was empty of any other visitors, just as he had promised. Lauren was relieved to find that Alex was just as easy to talk to as Christian.

They spent most of their time in the Art of the Americas section, which turned out to be Alex's favorite as well as Lauren's.

"I can't get into paintings," he admitted, as they circled a ten-foot totem pole from Alaska. "But I really like masks and weapons and all that Aztec and Inca stuff."

"Pre-Columbian art," Lauren said, leading him to two of the things she liked best in the whole museum: a Peruvian mini warrior, ornately carved and painted, crouched in the attack position, like some sort of vengeful elf, and a fragment of a stone carving representing the head of a god.

"It says the god is from Guatemala—from the fifth century! I can't believe it's so old," Lauren marveled.

"It's pretty weird-looking." Alex nodded, peering into the glass case. Lauren prickled with embarrassment. Maybe she shouldn't have raved about it so much. It was just an old piece of stone found in a jungle. She could just hear Ashley yawning. But so what? Girls like Ashley were lame. Besides, if Alex had been interested in a girl like Ashley, he would be dating one of the Ashleys, but he hadn't. He had asked her out.

But then . . . maybe he thought she *was* an Ashley because of the way she looked now. The old Lauren certainly wouldn't have attracted two lacrosse players to her side. Or would she have? Maybe it was just about confidence.

"We can go look at something else, if you want," Lauren said, backing away from the display.

Alex turned to look at her, his dark eyes intent and serious. "It's great that you're interested in, you know, *stuff*," he said. "Lots of girls can be so . . . I dunno. They're not like you. Most of them just giggle and want to hold hands."

Lauren returned his smile. She was right. He was interested in her—the real her—not the Ashley exterior. And the thought of holding hands with Alex made her feel weak at the knees. Literally. She might fall over at any second. She completely forgot about Christian. It was all about Alex right now.

"It's cool you know so much about things," he continued.

"Well, I don't know that much," she faltered. They were walking into the next room, but her eyes couldn't focus on anything. "And I like silly things as well."

"Yeah?" Alex asked, his voice playful.

"Yeah, like that new movie about those killer robots."

His face immediately lit up. "That movie's going to be awesome. Wanna go see it next week?"

"Sure!" Lauren nodded, completely forgetting that she had agreed to see the same movie with Christian just a few hours ago. She supposed she could live with seeing it twice.

She felt like skipping around the room. Christian and Alex were so nice! And they both wanted to see her again. . . .

One of these days she would have to decide which one she liked better. But not today, and not anytime soon.

LIGHTS. CAMERA. ASHLEYS!

"**H**URRY! YOU'RE THE LAST ONE TO ARRIVE!**"** Ashley pulled A.A. onto the overstuffed couch, where Lauren and Lili were already stationed, each girl balancing a small plate of goodies on her lap.

The brocade curtains were drawn in the Spencers' den, and the leather-covered coffee table was covered with white platters of pot stickers, mini burritos, and spring rolls, all made by the live-in gourmet chef. Ashley grabbed the remote, dinging it against the carafe of freshly squeezed lemonade. "The show's about to start."

The television set, a giant flat-screen above the fireplace, was tuned to the Sugar channel. The first episode of *Preteen Queen* was about to be broadcast, and Ashley couldn't wait. She'd had flyers made and distributed to every girl at Miss Gamble's, to make sure nobody missed the show. San

Francisco would be the first city shown, the producers had decided. There would be no more taping until the winners of the regional rounds went to New York. Their lives as reality-show vixens were over, but the fame was just about to begin.

Ashley wasn't the only one excited about this. As soon as the theme music began—"Just a Girl" by No Doubt—they all started squealing.

Omigod! There they were on the bench outside school, all looking supercute in their uniforms and Louboutin Mary Janes. The Ashleys were on national television! Her smile faded when she saw the others' dance-team rehearsal, but returned when she watched the next clip—there they were in Manners & Morals, explaining the rules of the Friendship Ceremony to all the nonfamous losers in their class!

It took about five seconds for excitement to turn into joy to turn into . . . well, disappointment. Was this what they really looked like? Ashley screwed up her face. She looked completely washed out, she decided. She was way too pale, almost sickly. She'd definitely have to ask for a darker spray tan next time.

But at least she didn't come over all whiny backstabber like Lili, who visibly squirmed when the producers asked her why she kept the dance-team performance a secret from Ashley.

"It wasn't like that!" Lili complained, pointing accusingly at the screen. "I mean—you were busy!"

Ashley didn't say anything, even though she was smirking inside. She'd played the whole thing expertly and had come out smelling like a rose—especially when she hugged the girls after they'd betrayed her.

And at least she had screen time, unlike Lauren. For half of the discussion on the bench scene, Lauren was cut out of the frame altogether. The big close-up was of A.A. protesting too much that she hadn't kissed dozens of boys. Then the screen showed the actual Friendship Ceremony.

"My singing voice is awful!" Lauren giggled. "I'm totally off-key!" Ashley had no idea why Lauren would think that was funny. But it was almost as if Lauren didn't care what she looked or sounded like on television.

"They keep zooming in on the bruise on my neck," complained Lili. "That's from playing the violin—it's not a hickey!"

"At least you don't look like a ditz," A.A. moaned. It was true: The way the show had been edited, A.A. was always staring into space, tapping her desk with a pencil, or examining her fingernails. And whenever she was shown applying lip gloss, the producers had added kissing noises on the soundtrack, reminding all the viewers that she was the one who liked to make out.

Ashley loved it. She couldn't wait for the last ten minutes of the show. She was the only one in this room who knew what was coming.

Then the screen changed, and Lili gasped. "Isn't that . . . isn't that the lacrosse party?" she asked, confused. "I recognize the spiral staircase! But how did they . . ."

The caption across the bottom of the screen flashed the words HIDDEN CAMERA FOOTAGE. The picture was jumpy and blurry, clearly taken with a small video camera. A Steadicam, maybe. Something hidden in a backpack, most likely.

"Oh God!" Lauren laughed as she nearly dropped her plate. "That's me standing in the corner by myself!"

The shot showed Lauren all alone, sipping her drink and gazing wistfully around the room. On the show's soundtrack, a solo violin played a mocking lament.

"Now where were the cameras when I was hanging out with those two guys?" she asked.

Ashley curled her lip. Lauren had told them she had met not just one, but two cute lacrosse players at the party, and had gone on dates with both of them last week. Not that any of them believed her, even though it was all over AshleyRank as well. Please. Lauren Page, man-killer? Ashley didn't think so. Lauren was *definitely* behind the blog, for sure. Besides, the cameras didn't lie. There she was looking like a huge loser as always.

"Oh well," Lauren said. "At least this way they won't know I'm dating both of them."

This girl really has an overactive imagination, Ashley thought. "Oh, there's me and Tri!" she said triumphantly. They were laughing and smiling at each other, and at one point Tri reached for Ashley's hand. How lucky that she was the only one with a boyfriend!

Onscreen the footage showed a closet door opening, and then A.A. stumbling out, followed by a redheaded guy with a sheepish look on his face.

"Who's that?!" Ashley shrieked. "A.A., you slut!"

"It's no one!" A.A. protested, looking pale. "I told you, I met some guy—a friend of Tri's—at the party. We hung out in the closet but nothing happened—I can't believe they're showing this part. We were only in there for a couple of minutes, and all we did was talk! But this makes me look so bad!"

Lauren and Lili consoled A.A., and Ashley made sympathetic noises as she snuggled into her cushion. A.A. was another one in dreamland. As if any girl would go into a closet with a guy just "to talk." Get serious! This was the best TV show she'd ever seen in her life. She hadn't had so much fun since Mischa Barton's character was killed off on *The O.C.*

"Omigod!" Now Lili was enraged. "They *di'in't!*"

The grainy footage showed Max pulling away from Lili in the butler's pantry. The dialogue was muffled, so the producers had helpfully provided the text at the bottom of the screen. "It's just weird." "What's weird?" "I'll see you around, okay?" Then Max abruptly left the pantry, walking away as fast as he could. The camera zoomed in on Lili look-ing shell-shocked, her eyes glistening with tears.

"God, Lil!" shrieked Ashley. "You never told us you cried!"

"Shut up!" Lili yelled, her cheeks aflame as she tried to smother Ashley with a tasseled pillow.

The other day Lili had finally confessed what happened the night of the party, and the Ashleys had a three-way con-ference call as Lili gave them the blow-by-blow of Max's mys-tifying hot-and-cold actions. Ashley was truly sympathetic but gratified that she was so lucky to have Tri, who would never do a thing like kiss her and then dump her all in the same second. She conveniently forgot about the fact that Tri had yet to express any interest in kissing her in the first place.

The hour-long show whizzed by, in Ashley's opinion, although A.A. was going on about it being the worst hour of her life. Ashley wished it was *longer*. Where was Tri? She couldn't believe he was missing her triumph. He said he was going to try and make it, even though he had something bor-ing and unimportant to do, like homework.

"Okay, is everyone ready to vote?" Ashley asked, picking up her phone, ready to dial. "Only one of us can go through to the next round."

All the girls grabbed their phones, dialing madly. Ashley was glad she'd told the house staff to watch on the kitchen television. They'd promised to vote for her many times. Of course, the other girls probably did the same with their familys' employees, but Ashley was counting on her household's many phone lines to tip the scales in her favor. Not that she was too worried. She definitely came across as the most likeable one.

"Hey—sorry I'm so late." The door creaked open, and Tri poked his head in.

About time! Ashley snorted. "Get your phone out!" she ordered. She'd have to be mad at him another time. Right now she needed him to cast a vote. Make that a hundred votes. "You have to keep dialing this number. I need you to vote as many times as possible."

"What am I voting for?" Tri sat at the end of the sofa, scratching his head.

"It's not *what*," Lili corrected him. "It's *who*."

"You're voting for me," Ashley informed him, raising her voice when Lili starting squealing in protest. "Get your own boyfriends if you want votes!" she said merrily.

"Which number . . ." Tri murmured, squinting at the split-screen images.

"A.A. is at the top," Lauren told him. Ashley rolled her eyes. Little Miss Helpful was just going to confuse him. Guys were *much* slower than girls when it came to the important things in life. "And then it's Ashley. And then it's—"

"Look—this is the number." Ashley walked over and thrust her phone in his face. "A.A. can ask that guy she made out with in the closet to vote for her. She doesn't need your vote."

"I already told you, I didn't make out with anyone." A.A. looked down and didn't meet Tri's eyes. She stared at her phone, pounding the keys.

"Really? That's unusual," Ashley said innocently, wriggling back into her seat. A.A. was in such denial! She could protest all she wanted that nothing had happened, but Ashley knew the truth. A.A. must think they were all born yesterday.

That secret party footage was a killer. It was sure to clinch the deal. Ashley was so glad she'd sent Jasper that text after the lacrosse games on Saturday with her latest brilliant brainwave, and that he'd been able to find a production intern willing and able to do the dirty work on such short notice. Everyone watching at home was sure to vote for Ashley now. Who wanted a wallflower, a slut, or a backstabbing meanie to be their Preteen Queen?

"Dial faster," she urged Tri. She noted with annoyance that he was staring intently at the screen, which was rolling credits while showing close-ups of the girls. His gazed lingered just a little too long on the shot of A.A. in her tiny dance-team uniform.

17

IT LOOKS LIKE TRI HAS NEVER HEARD OF REVERSE PSYCHOLOGY

A.A. DIALED SO MANY TIMES HER FINGERTIPS were numb. But it didn't matter. She knew that. Nobody would be voting for her, because that TV show made her look *awful*. Unlike Lili and Ashley, she didn't care very much about making it to the next round of the show, but she did care that she'd been made to look like a boy-crazy idiot on television. All the stuff filmed at school was bad enough, but the secret party footage was even worse.

Why wasn't there a camera in the supply closet as there was in the butler's pantry? Then everyone would see that she was telling the truth. But this way there was just her word against what everyone could see. Even if there had been a camera, the producers probably wouldn't use the footage anyway, A.A.

realized. They were looking for sleaze and scandal, not an innocent hug and a friendly conversation. She and Hunter had talked mainly about sports. But she had to admit Hunter was pretty cute, and when he asked for her number before they left the closet, she gave it to him.

That was all that happened.

But no one would ever believe her.

The whole world thought she'd made out with him.

Her face was crimson. There was no point in trying to avoid Ashley and Tri, anyway, not if she wanted to stay friends with them. Here she was in Ashley's den, with Ashley three feet away and Tri even closer. If she wasn't mistaken, he was actually leaning toward her.

"How come we never hang out anymore?" he muttered, not looking up from his phone. Any cessation in dialing activity would bring the wrath of Ashley down on his head.

"I don't know." She shrugged, a little surprised that he'd even noticed. "We're both kind of busy, I guess."

"You could come by tomorrow. I got the new Metroid Prime for Wii." He glanced up at her, his eyes hopeful.

A.A. shook her head. "Can't, I've got soccer practice," she said, even though she didn't. However much she wanted to stay friends with Tri, however much she missed the old, easy way they used to hang out, A.A. couldn't bring herself to say yes. Things had changed. He was Ashley's boyfriend. Just thinking about that made her feel queasy all over again. She stole a quick look at Tri. His mouth was set in a hard line.

"You know, you should be careful of that guy you were hanging out with at the party," Tri said softly.

"Which guy?" A.A. resented his tone.

"Hunter. The one you went into the closet with. Or didn't you bother to find out his name?" Tri flushed, and A.A. felt like smacking him. Since when was he so sarcastic and judgmental?

"Mind your own business," she snapped.

"Look, I'm just warning you. He just moved to our school, but everyone says he's a total dog when it comes to girls."

"Thanks for the warning, but I'd rather not take dating advice from a guy who lets his girlfriend boss him around all the time," said A.A., stabbing at the numbers on her phone to release her irritation. "And besides, I can take care of myself."

"What are you guys talking about?" Ashley called, in her bossiest this-is-my-house voice. "Tri, sweetie, are you voting for me?"

"Oh, he's voting for you, all right," replied A.A., and she bit her lip so hard she thought it might bleed.

She noticed that Tri gave her his most disgusted look as he inched away from her so he could sit closer to Ashley.

Who cared? He could keep his patronizing tone. That guy Hunter had been calling and texting her all week, and she hadn't replied. But now, thanks to Tri sticking his nose where he shouldn't, A.A. was sure of one thing.

As soon as she got out of Ashley's house, she was going to call Hunter back.

HERE AT THE RANK, WE'VE DECIDED TO OPEN THE POLLS. That's right. You can all get in on the action now. This is a democracy, darlings. Rate the girls! Vote for your favorites, just like a certain cable television show that aired the other night. We now have carpal tunnel from all that dialing!

So go ahead, you decide: Does Ashley deserve a 10 for Style, or is her recent foray into footless tights a fashion disaster? Does Lili merit a 2 for Smarts for how she handled the kiss-and-dump at the party? Does A.A. get a 9 for her sweet, heartbreaking Smile? Does Lauren deserve a 9 for Social Presence for her social-climbing agility? You decide!

We can't wait to find out who YOU think rules the school!

POWER TO THE PEOPLE?

ILI COULDN'T STAND IT.

She couldn't stand French, she couldn't stand Madame LeBrun's dowdy tweed skirt and sensible shoes, she couldn't stand having to drag herself to the Alliance Française every Monday afternoon—well, getting dragged there in her mother's SUV—and she couldn't stand the way Max was ignoring her.

This was their first attempt at Advanced French Conversation since the make-out/breakup session at the postgame party. The Monday following the party, Madame LeBrun had been ill and canceled class. Madame turned out to have a serious infection and class was canceled for a whole month. Total relief!

But this week she was back in her usual not-very-good health and had called Lili's mother to say she expected to see both her students. Lili tried to get out of it, but Nancy Khan closed that conversation down right away. Nobody in the Li household missed an appointment or skipped a class. The only excuse was dire illness, and Lili had never been any good at feigning sick. Her mother could see through ruses in a minute. And anyway, was she going to have to get a fever every Monday from now on? Her mother would never buy it.

Lili had been dreading French all day. What would Max say? Was he sorry at all about leaving her in the lurch? Did he even remember her since the party was weeks ago? Had he seen the whole humiliating scene play out on *Preteen Queen*, like every single girl at Miss Gamble's? Lili couldn't bear to think about that possibility. She'd even brought a box of tissues with her, so if Madame LeBrun had one of her manic sneezing fits, there'd be no excuse for the teacher to leave the room.

Lili arrived on time, as usual, and Max slouched in a few minutes later. He didn't even look at her. He just sat down, pulled his chair forward a little so he was closer to Madame LeBrun, and stared straight at the teacher. Not a hello, not a nod, not even an eyebrow raise. So this was how he was going to play it—just like a boy. Ignore it and it'll go away. How *humiliating*. Especially when she was the one being ignored.

Of all the things Lili was expecting Max to do or say today, him acting like he didn't even know her was at the bottom of the list. She felt just awful. So much for hoping that he regretted his rash decision to run off at the party. He was clearly determined to cut her out of his life totally, starting with his French conversation. Despite all Madame LeBrun's best efforts to get her two students to converse, Max directed all his questions and answers to the teacher. He just acted dumb when Madame tut-tutted about how he wasn't interacting with Lili. Anyone looking in at the class would think he hated her.

Hopefully, nobody was looking in. Lili couldn't be sure anymore, not since the producers pulled that hidden camera stunt at the party. Maybe Madame LeBrun was in on the conspiracy to humiliate her too. Why not?

The class was the longest hour of her life. As soon as Madame LeBrun told them they could go, Max grabbed his bag and skateboard and bolted down the stairs. That was *so* mature. If Max was incapable of acting in a civilized way, then it was just as well he wasn't Lili's boyfriend. She was never, ever going to a lacrosse game again.

By the time Lili followed Max down the stairs and out the doors—as slowly as possible, so Prince Not-at-All-Charming wouldn't think she was chasing him—and reached the car waiting for her, he was nowhere in sight. Good. Fine.

Lili stuck her nose in the air and climbed into the luxuriously padded backseat of the SUV. If that's how he wanted to play it, so could she.

Nothing in her life was going well at all. Since their episode of *Preteen Queen* had aired, all of the Ashleys were acting deflated and tired, like someone had let the air out of their balloons. The only person who was acting remotely perky was Lauren. What was up with that? Maybe she was so used to other people making fun of her that the TV show didn't seem so bad.

But for Lili and A.A., the whole thing had been a social disaster. Even Ashley, who should have been delighted that she came out of the whole thing so well, was instead nervous as hell, worrying about whether she'd won the vote tally. They wouldn't know until the following week, at the taping of the results party.

The SUV stopped at a light, and her Blackberry rang. She answered it. Ashley on the line. Maybe there was word about the show at last.

"BAD NEWS!" Ashley screeched in her ear.

"What? You didn't win? *Lauren* won?" Lili asked. She didn't see how Ashley could know the winner so early, but she wouldn't put it past her. Ever since her whole "hidden camera" trick, she seemed cozy with the producers. Maybe they'd spilled the beans.

"Forget about the show!" Ashley yelled. "I'm talking about the stupid blog. Can you believe the way *anyone* can destroy your average?"

Lili frowned. AshleyRank had recently gone interactive. Now it wasn't just the mysterious webmaster who decided rankings. Anyone could go online and rank you, ever since the blog had added a new pop-up "rank" window. So now even the most socially awkward, bitter girl in the school could rank you and it would affect your overall average. No wonder Ashley was freaking out.

"Are you saying I've gone *down* in the ranking?" Lili asked, not wanting to know the dreadful truth. She'd been exultant to find herself tied with A.A. the other week and worried about slipping into the number three position once again.

"Lil, not everything is about you, okay?" snapped Ashley. "Someone has *dared* to give me a 'two' for Smile—can you believe it? My number one spot is in peril! When I find out who did it, I'm going to make sure they never eat, drink, shop, or breathe in this town again!"

Lili suppressed a laugh. So Ashley's number one ranking was in danger? Maybe today wasn't so bad after all.

NEVER SAY NEVER

ASHLEY WAS TIRED OF ALL THE TALK about AshleyRank. Now that her numero uno position was in jeopardy, she had to start playing it down. That way, if the *unthinkable* happened and she dropped a notch—yikes!—then it was no biggie. She could shrug it off.

But at lunchtime in the ref, Lili kept bringing it up.

"Isn't it cool that seven new people gave me perfect tens in everything?" she squealed.

Ashley frowned. The way the rankings were going, Lili was going to speed ahead of A.A. and come dangerously close to striking distance on Ashley's title. She needed to change the subject pronto.

"So, girlies," she said. "Want to play a new game?"

"What?" A.A. looked up, interested. Even Lili was quiet. Lauren stopped licking her yogurt spoon and looked up. It was the first time Ashley noticed how Lauren was still hanging around, even though the show was pretty much over. She didn't know how she felt about that but decided it couldn't hurt to keep the charade going, at least until the results were revealed.

Ashley reached for her can of Red Bull. "It's called 'I Never,'" she explained. "We go around the group, and each person has to say something like 'I never pick my zits' or 'I never bite my cuticles.' If you're guilty of the crime—like if you *do* bite your cuticles—then you have to take a swig of your drink. You have to be totally honest, okay?"

"So if you were to say 'I never pick my zits' . . ." Lauren looked confused.

"Then I would have to take a drink." Ashley took a dainty sip of her Red Bull.

"And so would I," chimed in A.A., picking up her can.

"Me too." Lili sighed. She drank from her can, and Lauren, with a shy smile, followed suit.

"Your turn, Lil," said Ashley. Mission accomplished: Everyone had forgotten about AshleyRank.

"I've never spent more than three hundred dollars on shoes," said Lili with a smirk.

"Everyone's drinking to that!" A.A. predicted, and sure enough, each of the girls took a drink from their cans of Red Bull.

"How about . . . I've never thrown up my lunch," said Ashley. There was a pause, and then she picked up her can. "I know, gross, right? Barfing for beauty just isn't worth it."

She looked around and felt better when Lili picked up her can and took a sip. "It was totally ew," Lili confessed. "I'm never doing that again."

A.A. made a face but didn't pick up her can. Of course A.A. had never once thrown up her lunch, Ashley thought irritably: She had the metabolism of a boy!

Lauren hesitated, but finally she picked up her can. Well, well. Little Lauren wasn't such a Goody Two-shoes after all.

"I only did it to see if I could," Lauren said. "And you're right. It is totally disgusting."

"It's pathetic," Ashley declared. "Lauren, your turn."

"Um . . . I never watch *TRL*?" Lauren offered. That was the best she could come up with? Nobody even bothered picking up their cans.

"I've never kissed two guys on the same night," Ashley said, hoping Lauren would get the idea. The game was supposed to be way snarky. Otherwise, what was the point?

A.A. rolled her eyes and took another sip of Red Bull. She was the only one who did so, although Lauren looked like she was about to grab the can but then thought better of it. Well, A.A. could look as pissy as she wanted, Ashley thought. It was her fault for making out with guys all the time.

"A.A.'s turn," said Lili. God, she was so anal about turns! Ashley half expected Lili to draw up an agenda for the rest of the game. Luckily, there was only a minute of lunchtime left.

"Let me think," said A.A., drumming the top of her can with her French-polished nails.

"How about 'I've never embarrassed myself on national TV'?" groaned Lili. She checked her watch and picked up her bag. Lili could never bear to be late for class. Whereas Ashley didn't care. Class never started till she got there.

"I've got one," A.A. said, a closed look on her face. "I've never kissed a boy."

Ashley watched as A.A. picked up her can and took one long, final swig. Lauren flushed a pretty pink and picked up her can, drinking whatever was left. What? When did *she* kiss someone? Lili was busy drinking too. Well, at least they knew she wasn't lying this time. Unlike the Taiwan story, the one about her and Max was true. They'd all seen it on TV.

Ashley's hand gripped the can of Red Bull. The last thing she wanted to do was reveal her kiss-virgin status. But it was her game, and she knew the rules. You were supposed to be honest. Maybe she could just raise the can to her lips but not really drink . . . maybe that was okay?

The bell for afternoon classes rang. Saved!

Lili was already on her feet, hauling her bag off the floor, and Lauren was muttering about some boring

Honors class project she had to make a presentation for. Nobody seemed to notice that Ashley hadn't really drunk from her can.

Except for A.A., who was looking straight at her, not saying a word.

THE HEART IS DECEITFUL
ABOVE ALL THINGS

WHEN **A.A.** GOT HOME FROM SCHOOL that day, she headed straight for her bedroom and shut the door. Her mother was out somewhere—probably getting her Icelandic laser treatment or one of the Madagascan seaweed body wraps she swore by. Jeanine preferred beauty treatments, products, and therapies that came from another country, ideally somewhere super high-tech, tropical, or obscure.

She was always trying to drag A.A. to some New Age Sri Lankan spa in Russian Hill where they painted your chakra or tickled your aura or something. A.A. liked getting pedicures and massages, but her idea of relaxing wasn't getting pummeled with hot stones or listening to weird chants. She preferred blowing up a zombie head to release tension.

Kicking off her Mary Janes, A.A., nimble as a monkey, climbed the ladder to her loft platform bed and flopped down on the soft mattress. Her phone buzzed, alerting her to an incoming text message, but she ignored it. There were other things on her mind.

Ever since they'd been over at Ashley's to watch the disastrous *Preteen Queen* episode, when she snapped Tri's head off, he hadn't dropped by their penthouse apartment once. There was no point in prodding Ned for information. She was close to her stepbrother, but guys didn't like talking about feelings and relationships. And Ned was preoccupied at the moment with SAT stuff at school, and with training for the big track meets in the spring.

How could A.A. explain that because Tri was dating her best friend, she didn't feel comfortable hanging out with him anymore? That didn't make sense at all. Ned would shake his head and say it was all too much teen drama, as if he wasn't a teen himself.

Her school uniform was too uncomfortable for lounging around, especially the black tights that Ashley insisted they all wear this semester. A.A. slid back down the ladder and removed her uniform, leaving it on the floor, where the maid would rescue it for washing and ironing by Monday. She pulled on her favorite Nuala yoga pants and a soft cashmere sweater and thought about the game they had played at lunch.

Lili and Lauren may not have been paying attention, but A.A. was. Ashley had picked up her can but—and this was important—*didn't take a drink*. That meant only one thing—Ashley and Tri had never kissed!

They'd been going out for weeks and acting all lovey-dovey in the most barf-inducing way whenever they were seen in public. But "in public" was one thing. In private they clearly had no chemistry. Ha! A.A. didn't know why that gave her an odd sense of satisfaction, but it did.

And yet . . . what did it matter if Ashley and Tri kissed or didn't kiss? It was great to have something over Ashley for a change, but the feeling of triumph was hollow. Even if Ashley and Tri made out every day for an hour after school, it wouldn't affect A.A.—or it shouldn't affect her. It was their silly little relationship, and their business. She wanted Ashley to be happy, right? And God knows *she* didn't want to kiss Tri. Or . . . did she?

A.A. picked at a hangnail on her thumb. She had to be honest for once and admit what had been bothering her all this time. She'd been lying to herself for too long. The annoying truth was, she did like Tri. She'd liked him ever since she thought he was laxjock, but now that she thought about it, she'd liked him even before that.

He was sweet and goofy and the nicest boy she'd ever met. The way he looked at her with such intensity in his blue eyes, even when they were just making s'mores out of the microwave, gave her shivers. She'd been in love with him for so long she didn't even know it until he started going out with someone else and she was pierced with such exquisite jealousy she couldn't even function. Seeing them together was pure agony.

She didn't dare to hope what this no-kiss situation meant; she didn't want to get even more hurt than she was already. Even though Tri wasn't kissing Ashley, he was still technically her boyfriend, and it wasn't as if he was seeking A.A. out either. Except to give her some unwanted dating advice—the *nerve*. Either she was in love with him or she hated his guts, or a combination of the two.

Her phone buzzed again. A.A. sighed. It was probably just Hunter again. Ever since they'd met at the party, he'd been calling her every other day or so. After *Preteen Queen* aired, he'd even texted her. DON'T WORRY—THAT SHOW SUX! U + I KNOW THE TRUTH. HANG OUT 2MORROW?

Tomorrow came and went, but A.A. didn't see him. Then when he called again, A.A. had tried to make it clear she wasn't interested. In fact, she was totally blowing him off and hadn't returned any of his latest calls or texts. It wasn't really fair to Hunter. He hadn't done anything wrong. He was a nice guy. He had been good company in the closet.

What was her problem? Why was she still thinking about

Tri? He was off-limits. Whereas Hunter was available and more than eager to spend time with her.

She checked the last two texts. She was right, both were from Hunter. The first read: R YOU THERE? TALK 2 ME! The second was more to the point. 7 PARTY 2MORROW. BE THERE! BRING YE FRENZ.

Now this was interesting. Maybe it was time the Ashleys sampled the delights of a notorious "Seven Minutes in Heaven" party so they could see what it was really like.

A.A. was sure that none of the girls would be able to resist the invitation. Lili needed something to cheer her up after that humiliation with Max. Lauren was suddenly the party girl, always bringing up dates and boys, and Ashley . . . well, Ashley couldn't bear it if a party was going on and she wasn't all over it. Especially a party they'd been invited to by a cute boy.

Besides, maybe the only way to forget about someone was to kiss someone else. A.A. picked up her phone and replied to Hunter's message.

SURE! ME + 3. WHERE & WHEN?

21

THINGS THAT GO UP,
MUST COME DOWN

HE DOORS OF THE PRIVATE ELEVATOR THAT
led to A.A.'s penthouse apartment slid open, and
Lili stepped out. The Seven party was just six
hours away, and she didn't have anything to wear.

Shopping on a Saturday morning was impossible—she
had a tennis lesson immediately after breakfast, and then her
art appreciation class—but at tennis A.A. had told her not to
bother trawling the stores this afternoon. It was pouring
rain, and besides, A.A. had a closet full of things she never
wore. Lili could spend an hour or two in comfort, drinking
freshly squeezed melon juice and eating whatever she wanted
from the Fairmont's room service menu, trying on all of
A.A.'s clothes.

Because it was vital that Lili looked her best tonight. This was her first real social outing since the party after the lacrosse game, and she just knew people would be looking at her. Everyone she knew had seen her kiss Max and seen him dump her on national TV.

At school, Melody Myers had the whole hideous incident on DVD and she and her friends had replayed it, she told Lili, at least a dozen times to try and hear everything else Max was saying before he left the room. Thanks, Melody! Lili was fuming about that. She wished they'd never given Melody the SOA sticker last semester. Seal of Jealousy and Pettiness would have been more appropriate.

Lili didn't know if Max was going to be at the party tonight. She hoped not. But A.A. had convinced her that the best way to get over him was to go out and have some fun. Playing Seven Minutes in Heaven with some random boy— hopefully even cuter than Max—was just what the doctor ordered, A.A. insisted.

That way, Max wouldn't be the longest and greatest kiss of her life to date. He would be more like the boy in Taiwan, just one minuscule non-life-shattering experience on the path to grown-up romance. That sounded good to Lili. The sooner she could face Max—and his silent treatment in French every Monday—without feeling depressed and rejected, the better.

Lili found something she liked in A.A.'s closet—a tiny

pleated Alice + Olivia skirt and a ruffle-neck Geren Ford silk top. She tried them on and looked at herself in the mirror. "Can I borrow these?"

"Sure," A.A. called. "Have you checked AshleyRank today?" No other site mattered any more—not even MySpace or Perez Hilton.

"I haven't had time," Lili said, admiring the way the tiny skirt fit her slim figure. "This will look great with my new suede boots."

"News flash—Ashley got another bad anonymous ranking." A.A. rolled to the edge of her bed and gazed down at Lili with a wide grin.

"No!"

"Yes! Someone gave her a three for Smarts." A.A. snickered.

"Oh." Lili was a little disappointed. A three for Style or even Social Presence would have been much worse. Ashley didn't really care about smarts, as long as everyone thought she was beautiful and popular. "Who do you think runs that blog, anyway? Do you think it's really Lauren?"

"Ashley thinks so. She's like ninety-nine percent sure that Lauren is the brains behind it."

"I guess." Lili sighed, and did another twirl.

"But you know what this means," A.A. pointed out, dangling her long, slender arms over the side of the bed. She'd had a manicure, Lili noticed—maybe she liked this guy Hunter after all. A.A. had never paid any attention to stuff like that too much before. "This three for Smarts score."

"What? That someone thinks Ashley is at second-grade reading level? So what?"

"Think about it. Ashley can't stay number one for much longer. You don't have to be a math genius to work that one out. One more bad score could bring her average *way* down. And you know what that means. . . ."

Lili gasped.

A.A. waggled her eyebrows. "She'll lose her crown," she said, saying exactly what Lili was thinking. "And then . . ."

"Someone else will take the number one spot!" Lili spun around, stamping her foot and clutching her skirt as though she were a flamenco dancer. "I can't wait!"

22

YOU HAVE TO BE CRUEL TO BE KIND

LAUREN WAS NERVOUS. DASHING BETWEEN DOWN-pours in and out of the boutiques along Maiden Lane, she felt her stomach twisting into knots of tension. A.A. had invited her to a party tonight, her second real party. And not just any party—her first Seven party. As in "Seven Minutes in Heaven." Not that she had to play. A.A. said participation was entirely optional.

But that wasn't why she was so nervous.

This morning, both Christian and Alex had sent her text messages. That party Christian mentioned at the end of watching the killer robot movie? It was the party she was going to with the Ashleys. And that party Alex had talked about during their date? Oh yeah . . . it was the very same event.

She had two sort-of potential future boyfriends, and they both saw tonight's get-together as their sort-of-third date with her. What was she going to do? She didn't want to play it safe and stay home. That's what the old Lauren would have done. The old Lauren wouldn't have a single boy interested in her, let alone two really cute lacrosse players.

She wanted to go to the party, and she wanted to see Christian and Alex again. But Lauren didn't want to expose herself as a double-dater or make them feel like she was playing them off against each other. And she really didn't want them to get annoyed with her for being a liar—a little white liar, but still—and dump her. She'd had a good time with both of them.

It was so confusing: Did she like Christian best or Alex? Christian was so cute and funny, and really easy to talk to. Lauren didn't feel like she had to put up a front when she was with him. Alex was more serious, even though he was just as hot. She'd loved looking around the museum with him. Maybe tonight would help her decide which boy she should spend more time with. Being on the brink of having an actual boyfriend was scary and exciting. That's why she was out shopping now, despite the torrential rain and gusty wind, to buy something irresistibly gorgeous.

In the Ted Baker store, it took Lauren only ten minutes to go through the new fall line and decide that there was nothing for her to wear to the party. Once the rain stopped, she was going to make her way to the next store. Or maybe she should just call Dex and ask him to come pick her up. Sometimes shopping wasn't that much fun, no matter how much money you had to spend, especially if you didn't have any friends with you.

She was just about to give up when the heavy velvet curtain of one of the bedroom-size changing rooms opened, and Ashley, wearing a simple sweater and a pair of skinny jeans, stepped out. The changing room looked like a bomb had hit it—clothes lay all over the armchair and floor where Ashley had discarded them. Her pale, pretty face broke into a smile when she spotted Lauren standing by the rack of black pants.

"God! Can you believe this place?" she complained, taking Lauren's elbow in a really friendly way. Ashley was always nicer when Lili and A.A. weren't around. "Everything is so *middle-aged*. They used to have cute stuff here, but I couldn't find a thing today, unless I want to look like Hillary Clinton."

"I couldn't find anything either," Lauren confided.

"You want something for the party tonight, right?" Ashley looked sympathetic. "What kind of look are you going for?"

"I don't know. Not too dressy, but not casual, either. Maybe I need to go to Neiman's and speak to my personal shopper." Lauren wasn't entirely confident about putting clothes together yet. Unlike the Ashleys, she was still new to this buy-anything way of life.

"You don't need a personal shopper when *I'm* here,"

Ashley said, flicking her shiny blond hair out of her face. "Let's get out of this store and go somewhere else. I'll find the perfect outfit for you."

Lauren agreed at once. This was an unexpected bonus: getting quality time with Ashley. She seemed less affected than she did at school, more human almost. Ashley's driver was waiting outside in her father's tan Range Rover, and he drove them to Union Square. There, in less than an hour, Ashley had found more than a dozen amazing things at Saks for Lauren to try on.

In the shoe department, Ashley insisted that Lauren look for a pair of strappy, studded high heels, because that's what all the coolest celebrities were wearing.

"I don't want the heel to be too high," said Lauren, tugging on a pair of Jean-Michel Cazabats and thinking about Alex. He was taller than her, but not that much taller—she didn't want to tower over him tonight. Ashley obviously didn't care about being taller than Tri. Lauren wished she had her confidence.

"Your school shoes are higher than this," Ashley pointed out with a dismissive wave. Then she looked hard at Lauren, her lip curling into a smirk. "Oh, I get it. You're worried about being taller than the boys at the party."

"No! I mean . . . maybe." Lauren slumped in the chair, hoping that Ashley wouldn't tease her too much. "Well, there is this one boy I like who might be there. . . ." She knew Ashley didn't believe she was dating two boys, so she didn't want to bring that part up.

"Is he short like Tri?" Ashley looked sympathetic.

"No, not . . . " Lauren was about to say "not *that* short" but stopped herself in time. "He's just not *really* tall."

"Hmmm." Ashley pondered the problem. Lauren couldn't believe that Ashley wasn't grilling her, mocking her, or dismissing the entire issue outright. She looked like she was seriously pondering Lauren's dilemma. "I'm trying to come up with the most . . . you know, *intelligent* solution."

That was kind of a weird thing to say, but Lauren sat silently, waiting for Ashley's verdict.

"I've got it!" Ashley clicked her fingers. "Buy these Michael Kors strappy wedges, because they have only a one-and-a-half-inch heel. Then—and this is the masterstroke, if I do say so myself—team them with that Stella McCartney short skirt and Rachel Pally kimono top. The skirt will make your legs look superlong even without a really high heel. You'll be the cutest girl at the party!"

"That'll be great," Lauren agreed, smiling at Ashley. So this was why the Ashleys stayed friends—despite all of Ashley's machinations and mean tricks. Under the Queen Bee facade was a really nice person all along.

"I mean, most of the girls at the party will be ugly and/or

skanky, and very badly dressed," Ashley continued, handing the box with the approved shoes to the hovering sales assistant. "The only possible competition you have is the Ashleys, and you have nothing to worry about there. Lili is so petite she's almost a midget, and A.A. is freakishly tall. She'd make out with a vacuum cleaner if she thought it was taller than she was."

Okay—so Ashley wasn't *that* nice. But she was being nice to Lauren for a change, and that felt good. Lauren felt a tiny bit guilty about wanting to be Ashley's friend only so she could take her down in the future. This was all so confusing. Was Ashley mean or nice? Did she like Ashley or did she loathe her? Things were a lot more complex than Lauren had first thought.

"What about you?" Lauren asked, wanting to stop thinking about her conflicted feelings toward her new style guru. "You'll be wearing something amazing as usual, I'm sure."

"Yeah," Ashley agreed. She sighed and picked at a loose thread in the arm of her chair. "But I'm not going tonight."

"No?"

"Tri told me he can't, so what's the point? I need to go stay home and deep-condition my hair anyway. Besides, I want my first kiss to be something special, not just because we got shoved in a closet together."

"What do you mean, your first kiss?" Lauren couldn't believe what she was hearing. "You mean you and Tri haven't . . . ?"

"Nope. I'm NBK. Never Been Kissed. It's no biggie."
Ashley shrugged.

"Really?"

"Of course not. That's why I've been making Tri wait. I'd
rather wait until the moment's right. My parents always told
me that I'm like a precious jewel, and there's no point in—
how does that old saying go? No point in casting pearls
before swine or something?"

"That's so cool," Lauren told her. She almost felt guilty
for wanting to kiss both Christian and Alex. After Ashley's
confession, she wanted to tell her something in return,
because they'd been bonding so well that afternoon. "You
know, I'm NBK as well," she confided.

"Really? But when we played 'I Never' the other day, and
A.A. asked that question, you took a drink!"

"I just held the can to my mouth," whispered Lauren. "I
didn't want to look stupid."

"You really shouldn't lie," Ashley said, her face stern.
Then she was smiling again. "But it's okay. It's just a game.
Your secret's safe with me. I'm the most discreet of the
Ashleys, by the way, in case you hadn't noticed."

Lauren hadn't noticed. But she nodded and smiled back
at her new BFF, and they walked over to the counter together
to pay for her new shoes.

HUNTER PLANS A HOOKUP

AS SHE SURVEYED THE SCENE, **A.A.** THOUGHT that the location for the Seven Minutes in Heaven party wasn't quite as cool as the triplex loft after the lax game. It was in some guy's basement in Noe Valley. But even basements in this area were pretty nice, given the size of the houses and the amount of money everyone lavished on them.

This basement was particularly choice, furnished with a sofa, plush giant bean bags, a Perspex sling-chair hanging from the ceiling, a huge flat-screen TV and stereo system, and a pool table covered in purple felt. There were two bathrooms, two bedrooms, and even a kitchenette with a microwave and fridge, fully stocked with every type of salty snack, cereal, and candy.

There was a table set up for poker, already encircled with boys, as well as two pinball machines and a foosball table.

There were a bunch of closets in the back with white double doors. And their host for the evening—a Gregory Hall kid called Denver or Portland or some other city name—had gone to the trouble of hanging little VACANT/OCCUPIED signs on each of the door handles, just in case anyone forgot the point of the party.

A.A. arrived with Lili, who was checking herself out in every available surface to see how cute she looked in A.A.'s clothes. They got themselves sodas and talked to a few people they recognized. Ashley hadn't arrived yet, and A.A. couldn't see Lauren anywhere either. Lili, she knew, kept anxiously scanning the room for any sign of Max. She had told A.A. she both wanted and didn't want him to be there.

She felt bad for Lili, especially because some of the girls were still whispering and giggling about the hidden camera footage in the *Preteen Queen* broadcast. Jealous losers! They would faint in a heap if someone like Max even *looked* at them, which he would never do. She felt proud of Lili for brazening it out, telling those gossip-mad wenches that she'd been acting up for the camera, but nobody really believed her.

A.A. spotted Tri, playing pool in the back corner. She was a little surprised to see him. He had come over to their penthouse suite earlier with Ned and a bunch of other guys. She'd mentioned she was going to be at the party, and he said he wasn't planning to be there.

So what was he doing there, then? Ugh. As soon as Ashley arrived, the two of them would be all over each other as usual. A.A. didn't intend to run away this time, but she didn't want to witness any more of their PDA. Maybe they hadn't kissed, but they sure couldn't keep their hands off each other.

"You made it." Hunter sidled up next to her and leaned against the kitchen counter. A.A. smiled at him. He wasn't bad to look at, she supposed. Red hair, green eyes, and a kind-of-dashing cleft in his chin. Taller than her. Not bad at all. Did she want to spend seven minutes making out with him? Maybe. Maybe not.

"Did you meet my friend Lili?" A.A. made the introductions, pointedly ignoring the Ashley wannabes staring at Hunter so hard their eyes were about to fall out. Hunter took her elbow and led her away from the gaggle, bending toward her to whisper in her ear.

"Get out your phone," he murmured.

"Why? Have you sent me a message?"

"No. Just let me see it."

"It's an iPhone."

Hunter sighed and shook his head.

"Why do you have to make everything so difficult all the time?" he asked her, clearly trying not to laugh. A.A. didn't know what he was talking about.

"This is it, if it means so much to you." She slid her

iPhone out of her Mulberry shoulder bag and held her palm out so Hunter could see.

"Cool." He stared down at it. A.A.'s mom had had her iPhone bedazzled with rhinestones by some celebrity phone "customizer." A.A. thought it was silly to pay someone a ton of cash just to ruin the back of your phone, but she hadn't been able to stop Jeanine.

"You haven't seen an iPhone before?" A.A. was incredulous.

"I haven't seen *your* iPhone," he whispered. "Or felt it. Don't you know the rules of 'Seven'?"

A.A. shook her head.

"All the girls put their phones into a big bowl. That one over there"—he gestured with his left shoulder—"on the coffee table. When a guy's ready to play, he finds the Bowl-master. See that dude there in the T-shirt?"

A.A. followed his gaze. A guy with an almost-shaved head, wearing a T-shirt with a goldfish bowl drawn on it in crude black lines, was stationed in the swinging Perspex chair.

"He blindfolds you, and then you get to fish a phone out of the bowl. After that, you take off the blindfold and then you have to cruise the party to find the girl who owns it. Kind of like Cinderella with the glass slipper. You *have* heard of Cinderella, haven't you?"

"Ha-ha." A.A. rolled her eyes. This all sounded pretty

exciting. But what if the guy who grabbed your phone was fugly? She glanced around the room, checking everyone out. Nobody here was *too* bad. And at least it would be dark in the closet.

"When he finds you, you have to go into the closet with him and spend seven minutes there. Ideally not just because you're hiding from someone else." Hunter nudged her.

"Uh-huh." A.A. smirked. Hunter was a terrible flirt.

"If you drop your phone in the bowl, it means you want to play. So think about it before you back out like a baby," he teased.

"Like you're so mature," A.A. said, nudging him back even harder. "You haven't even seen an iPhone before."

"You're not listening to me, are you?" Hunter feigned exasperation. "I wanted to feel your phone because I knew you'd have some girly stuff hanging on it or whatever. You've got those diamonds stuck to it, right? So when I've got a blindfold on and I'm sticking my hand into the bowl, I'll know what to reach for. Got it now?"

"Oh." A.A. realized what he was saying and felt her face flush. Hunter wanted to make out with her. In the closet. For seven minutes. It was kind of flattering to see how determined he was to pick the right phone.

"This is just for your sake, you understand," he told her with a sarcastic grin, his eyes twinkling. "I don't want you stuck with some kid with braces or a major case of acne. I'm prepared to bite the bullet—you know, suffer through seven minutes with you in a closet—just so you're not traumatized. You should really be thanking me."

"Let's wait until the seven minutes are up, shall we?" A.A. flashed back at him.

"Bowl's right over there," he responded breezily, walking away.

A.A. fingered her phone, wondering what to do.

Maybe, maybe not. Maybe . . . why not?

She noticed a commotion around the pool table: Tri had sunk the winning shot and was being slapped on the back by the rest of his team. He looked incredibly happy, maybe because he was good at something for once, she thought nastily. All her annoyance at him returned in full force. Mustering her courage and trembling with a strange sort of exhilaration, she marched over to the glass bowl, already half full, and slid her phone in. She wanted to play.

24

IN A GAME OF CLUE, LAUREN HOPES NOT TO BE CLUELESS

T WAS JUST LIKE HER FAVORITE BOARD GAME, Lauren thought. There was Christian, in the living room, with the pool cue. And then there was Alex, in the bedroom, with the foosball table. And then there was Miss Page, moving from one room to the other, hoping her sneaking back and forth would go undetected. Someone was going to be onto her before long. But until that happened, she was going to have a really good time.

This was a problem she'd never experienced in her life before. How to hide the fact that she was dating two boys from the two boys she was dating? Madness. Complete and utter madness.

In the bedroom, during a break in the complicated pool tournament the boys had set up, she stood in a corner with Alex. Make that very, very close to Alex. The room was packed with players and spectators, as well as a steady stream of couples going in and out of the closet, so getting pressed up against him was inevitable. Being this close to Alex was thrilling. No other word for it. And when, midway through a sentence, trying to make himself heard over the music and the shouting, he bent his head down so their foreheads were touching, Lauren almost gasped with excitement.

But there was no time to gasp, or anything else, because he kissed her.

Lauren Page had been kissed by a really cute boy. And not because she'd dumped her cell phone in a bowl. Because he liked her and wanted to kiss her.

She was afraid she was going to melt into a puddle on the floor at any second.

"I'm sorry," Alex mumbled, stepping back a little and smiling sheepishly.

"Don't be," she said quickly. "I mean, it was nice."

What a stupid thing to say! "Nice." Is that all she could come up with?

"I kind of thought so too," he said, his dark eyes boring into hers. Lauren wanted to shriek with happiness.

"Alex—you're up!" Another boy walking past slapped him on the shoulder. "Quarterfinals, dude!"

"Sorry," he told her. "I can drop out of this stupid tournament if you like."

"No, no," she reassured him. "You go ahead. I need to go find my friend . . . Lili. She has this big story she wants to tell me. I'll come back here and find you, okay?"

"Don't run away," he said, squeezing her hand. *Oh my God!* She'd just kissed Alex and then lied to him. She was the Mata Hari of Miss Gamble's. She might have to be put to death by firing squad when all her sneaky behavior was revealed, just like in that old black-and-white movie she saw with her mother one afternoon.

In the living room she found Christian leaning on his pool cue. His dreamy face cracked into a big puppy-dog grin when he saw her walking over.

"I was wondering where you were hiding," he said, ruffling her hair so it was almost as messy as his. "You haven't been climbing into a closet with anyone, have you?"

"Oh, no," Lauren said, widening her eyes. That was true. No closet required. She and Alex had kissed in public. But no need to bother Christian with all the gory details . . .

"So." He looked down at his shoes and then back up at her. "What do you say we give this Seven game a whirl? See if it's as fun as everyone says."

"You mean . . . ?" Lauren wasn't sure if she was hearing right. It was bedlam in this room. Christian gestured with his left shoulder toward a closet. The sign read VACANT.

"Do you want to? 'Cause if you don't, it's okay. I just wondered . . ."

"It's okay," she said without thinking. Christian looked so adorable, so hopeful. How could she resist him? It was only seven minutes, after all. "I was wondering as well."

Miss Page, in the closet, with Crush Number Two.

Thank God there weren't TV cameras at *this* party.

SEVEN MINUTES IN . . . WHERE?

LILI DIDN'T FEEL LIKE PLAYING SEVEN MINUTES in Heaven. All she wanted to do tonight was avoid Three Hours of Hell. And her idea of hell was being at a party—any party—where Max was anywhere in sight.

She was sitting as elegantly as she could manage on one of the squishy, eggplant-colored beanbags splattered around the basement's largest room, half listening to some girl on an adjacent beanbag dish about the last Seven party she'd attended. Every ten minutes or so the Bowlmaster led a blindfolded guy over to the bulbous glass bowl on the coffee table and watched while he fished out a cell phone. Lili shivered. That wasn't her idea of fun.

She didn't have A.A.'s nerve. Judging by the number of phones crammed in the bowl, Lili didn't have the courage of half the girls here tonight. After kissing Max at the last party,

Lili had no interest in making out with anyone else for a long time. Maybe never. She'd really liked kissing Max, and he seemed to like kissing her. That is, until he freaked out and ran away. Lili didn't want to risk that happening again, so her cell phone was staying safely inside her bag tonight.

It must have been at least half an hour since A.A. had dropped her phone in the bowl, but she hadn't been "claimed" by anyone yet. Lili could see her sitting on the kitchenette's counter, chatting away with a couple of other girls from Miss Gamble's. The girls may have been willing, but it looked like the boys were more hesitant to really get Seven Minutes going. Typical! Ashley was right: Boys were so slow.

Ashley herself was AWOL. Lili had sent her a couple of texts, and Ashley had responded that she was busy washing her hair. Yeah, right. Ashley probably just wanted to make a grand entrance as usual. Tri was at the party, playing pool and looking pretty cute. Ashley had better get herself down here pronto if she didn't want her boyfriend lured away by one of these Seven-playing hussies.

Lauren had arrived, looking amazing in her dress and strappy wedges. Damn, that girl looked good! Ever since she'd started hanging with the Ashleys, she was looking more and more put-together.

The folks at AshleyRank had certainly noticed. Thinking

of AshleyRank made Lili sit up a little straighter, clamp her knees together a little more firmly, and smile at the girl next to her, who was talking a little more brightly. Now that anyone could vote, the world had to see that Lili was the superior Ashley. She totally deserved to be number one.

Something was up with Lauren tonight. First of all, Lili saw her talking to one of the lax players—that one with the messy hair and the dimples. Christian, maybe? They were huddled in one corner for a while, and it looked like he was hanging on her every word. Then Lauren was in *another* huddle with Dark and Handsome over by the pool table. Well, she wasn't lying after all! Lauren was Miss Popularity! Well, as long as Lauren steered clear of a certain Reed Prep player, Lili didn't mind.

Max Costa. Max Costa. She *had* to stop obsessing over him. It was silly: She'd almost forgotten him, really. He was out of her mind. Totally out of it. At French conversation class, Lili felt as indifferent to him as she used to feel to slacker Greg. Max was just some lame jock with a big ego. If he hadn't called a halt to their relationship-in-progress, she would have ended it herself, probably that night. There were so many more attractive and available fish in the sea. Next!

Lili scanned the basement, looking for a better prospect. Maybe she would drop her cell phone in the glass bowl after all. Or maybe she'd take a leaf out of Lauren's book and just work the room. If boys liked Lauren, they'd love Lili. She was still ahead of Lauren in the ranking. She shouldn't waste another second of her life thinking about Max.

Then she saw him.

He was walking down the stairs that led into the basement's living room. His blond hair was slicked back, and he was wearing a dark brown button-down shirt—the same cocoa color as his eyes—over a pair of faded jeans. His expression was kind of anxious and preoccupied, as though he wasn't really happy to be there.

Not that Lili was staring at him.

She shrank back into her beanbag, wishing it would swallow her up. Max stepped into the room and turned, obviously waiting for someone else coming down the stairs. A tall girl with curly brown hair, smiling like a dumb Tiara Girl. Lili had met her at the last party: She was a seventh grader at Reed Prep, Max's school, which was coed. Her name was Holly or Polly or Dolly or something.

Holly or Polly or Dolly had said that she was glad she went to Reed Prep because she couldn't believe how unbelievably boy-crazy the girls she met from all-girls schools could be. She herself didn't see what the big deal was about having a boyfriend.

But Lili noticed bitterly how Holly or Polly or Dolly extended a slender hand to grab Max's arm, like a bird of prey wrapping its talons around a victim, and beamed a triumphant smile. Sure, it wasn't a big deal at all.

Lili's stomach felt like a concrete mixer, churning with sludge. Her eyes prickled with tears. The sight of Max at the party with another girl was devastating. Her evening was over. She had to get out of there.

26

RULES ARE MADE TO BE FOLLOWED

A.A. HAD LOST SIGHT OF HUNTER: HE was embroiled in a poker game in another room and seemed to have forgotten all about playing Seven Minutes in Heaven. Lili had already gone home. One look at Max and his smirking date, and Lili had called her driver and asked to be picked up right away. A.A. told her she'd stick around for a little longer.

When Lauren seemed to disappear as well, A.A. was the last Ashley in the room, but that was okay. She played two games of pool with some of Ned's friends, studiously avoiding any conversation with Tri. It was so embarrassing because she sucked at pool, and he kept looking over at her like he was desperate to talk to her. Maybe to give her tips on her form. Or maybe it was just because Ashley wasn't here, she guessed. Too bad—she wasn't an Ashley substitute.

But when she walked over to the kitchenette to get

another soda, Tri followed her, obviously determined to get her attention.

"Do you want a drink?" she asked him, holding up the Diet Pepsi bottle and swinging it in front of him. "Or are you just following me to make sure I don't go off with any guys I can't handle? I know you're a *much* better judge of character than I am."

Tri looked down, not managing to hide his shamefaced grin.

"You're still mad at me about what I said?" he asked, his bright blue eyes glancing up at her.

A.A. shrugged. It was hard to stay mad at Tri, especially when he looked so cute. And she knew, in her heart of hearts, why she was really mad at him, but she couldn't tell him that.

"Good." He looked relieved. "Because that would make this even more awkward."

"What?" A.A. slung the bottle back into the mini-fridge and turned to face Tri. "This party?"

Tri shook his head.

"No, I mean . . ."

"What?" she asked again. What was wrong with this boy? He couldn't even finish a sentence since Ashley had gotten her hands on him.

Tri said nothing at all: He simply held up a cell phone. *Her* cell phone.

"I pulled it out of the bowl," he told her. "I knew it was yours before I even got the blindfold off."

"The rhinestones," she said quietly, her heart beating faster.

"Yeah. So, you know. We have to go into the closet. The Bowlmaster's watching."

They both looked over at the guy in the Perspex chair. He saluted them and pointed to the nearest closet. The sign on the door read VACANT.

"He's kind of a stickler for tradition," Tri said, his voice apologetic.

"Well," said A.A., her heart racing and her mouth dry. *What about Ashley?* she wanted to ask. *Your girlfriend? My best friend?* But maybe it didn't matter, because it was only a stupid game. It didn't mean what she thought it meant. All they had to do was sit around in a closet for seven minutes. She could do that. "Then I guess we have to."

"Yeah." He nodded, not meeting her gaze. "I guess we do."

Tri led her into the big double closet, turning the sign to OCCUPIED before closing the door. It was so dark in there that she almost tripped on something before Tri steadied her with a hand on her elbow.

Unlike the last closet A.A. had found herself in, this one was empty apart from two cushions on the ground.

"Very thoughtful," she said, sitting down on one and

scooting over so Tri could sit down next to her. She had this sudden nervous urge to talk. "Unless this is what they use their closets for—you know, to keep cushions in. Which doesn't make sense at all. I mean, who has extra cushions?"

He chuckled, and the noises of the party were muffled, but A.A. felt like the loudest sound in the closet was her pounding heart. They were alone together in the dark. The two of them had been alone before—countless times, just hanging out in her room, but never like this. She pulled her knees up to her chin. She liked it inside the closet; it felt warm and cozy sitting next to Tri. She had really missed him.

"So how do you like the new version of Metroid Prime? Is it everything they said it would be?" she asked.

"Yeah, it's pretty cool. My brother got us a subscription to a multiplayer Wii channel. It rocks. You should get one— we can team up maybe."

"Sure, why not?" They talked a little more about video games and the latest episode of *Cheaters*, which neither of them was allowed to watch but did anyway. A.A. started to relax and enjoy his company. She'd almost forgotten the reason they were sitting in the closet, when Tri reached over and put his hand over hers.

"A.A." His voice was soft.

"Yeah?"

"I don't think we're supposed to spend seven minutes *talking*. . . ."

"Oh . . ," A.A. tried to keep the panic out of her voice. She'd known Tri *forever*. "You mean we just sit here in silence?" He wasn't thinking what she was thinking, was he? How could he? He had a girlfriend! Who was Ashley. What was she doing in here with someone else's boyfriend? A.A. felt confusion and excitement and guilt.

"Well, technically, we have to kiss," said Tri, and now he sounded nervous as well. "Those are the rules of the game."

"I know," A.A. said. She'd wanted to play. Besides, it was just a seven-minute-long game that involved kissing. Kissing Tri. *Omigod!* Is that what he wanted them to do? He had pulled her phone out of the bowl—but what about Ashley . . . but all thoughts of Ashley, and all the guilt she felt, disappeared when she looked at Tri.

Her eyes had adjusted to the darkness and she could see he looked exactly the way she was feeling. Nervous, and shy, and . . . eager. He wanted this too, she could tell. Maybe this even meant he felt the same way about her? She felt a wild, reckless happiness.

"I mean, unless you really don't want to," he said.

"No," she said quickly, giving his hand a squeeze. "I mean, yes. What I mean is, we really should. I mean, it's the rules and all," she said, as if that were the most sensible thing to do. They couldn't disappoint the Bowlmaster, could they?

"It's the rules," he agreed, and even in the dark she could see Tri's face leaning toward her. She closed her eyes, and he pulled her closer so she pressed against him and felt the galloping beat of his heart. It was pounding even more loudly than hers.

Then she turned her face to his and felt the heat of his breath just before his soft lips touched her own.

Ashley would have to understand, they were just following the rules of the game . . . it didn't mean anything.

Still, it was the sweetest—and most amazing—seven minutes of her life.

WE'RE EXPERIENCING SOME TECHNICAL DIFFICULTIES here at the Rank. Bear with us as we crunch the numbers on this week's tally. Since opening the floodgates, we've been swamped by legions of new rankings, and we promise to post the new pecking order as soon as our server is back online.

In the meantime, put another layer of Glossimer on your lips, slip on your sweetest pair of Genetic jeans, and strut like you own this town. The whole world is watching and ranking your every move. . . .

27

GENTLEMEN PREFER BRUNETTES

NORMALLY ASHLEY SPENT SUNDAY MORN-
ing in bed, picking at the breakfast deliv-
ered to her on a white-clothed tray—scrambled
egg whites with a fruit cup and a bowl of soy latte, prepared
by their live-in chef—and watching an *America's Next Top
Model* or *Project Runway* marathon on the flat-screen TV
above her antique dresser.

Her parents would wander in occasionally to kiss the
top of her head, or to tell her about some dull story from
the Sunday *Chronicle*, or to retrieve the Style section when
she was finished picking it apart. She'd lie there in her
Limited Too PJs and fluffy slippers, playing with Princess
Dahlia von Fluffsterhaus, her labradoodle puppy, sending
texts to the other Ashleys, and thinking over important
long-term plans. Like: They all needed a new handbag next
semester. And the black tights were getting old. Should

they do knee-high argyle socks and Prada saddle bags?

But today was different. The big live results party for *Preteen Queen*, when the winner of the San Francisco episode would be announced—and her reaction filmed for the next round—was scheduled for Wednesday night. There were going to be five of these parties going on simultaneously around the country, so all the winners were announced at once. All this meant was extra pressure on Ashley to look fabulous.

She had spent most of the morning rehearsing what she'd do when her name was called. She didn't want to cry in an unflattering way, sobbing like a Miss America contestant. She had to achieve the right mix of joy, hysteria, false modesty, and fake surprise, all while looking cute. It had to all seem spontaneous as well, which was the hardest thing.

And, of course, she had to have the perfect dress to wear. Preferably one that worked with her blue animal-print Louboutin high heels, the ones she'd seen Heidi Klum wearing. Today would be dedicated to rampaging on a search-and-destroy mission through her mirrored walk-in closet and dressing room, trying on every possible look and deciding if she needed something new.

When her name was announced as the regional winner of *Preteen Queen*, Ashley had to look perfect. But there were only so many hours in the day for shopping once boring old school had sucked up half of it. Maybe Ashley could persuade her mother to let her take Tuesday off. She needed a haircut, a facial, a massage, an eyebrow wax, and a mani/pedi.

The party had to start at five, just like the one in L.A., because of stupid Pacific time: The New York and Miami parties were all starting at eight, while Dallas's began at seven, and the producers wanted the parties to be simultaneous. There was barely enough time after school to get her makeup professionally done and her hair blown out. Oh well, Ashley thought—this was what actresses had to go through for the Oscars every year, getting ready in the middle of the after-noon for a big evening event. The only difference was, they didn't have to waste the whole day at Miss Gamble's.

The other thing complicating today's schedule was Tri. He'd sent her a text to ask if he could come over to talk, and she'd agreed at once. They had *so* much to discuss. He was her date, and he had to live up to the image. He couldn't just arrive at the party wearing his Gregory Hall uniform or—even worse— jeans and a T-shirt, no matter how cute he looked in them.

Their outfits needed to complement each other, without looking all matchy-matchy in a suburban–old couple–tourist sort of way. Maybe she could talk him into a haircut as well. Ashley could be very persuasive when she tried. She was used to telling people what to do.

The butler ushered Tri into her room not long after she replied to his text message. He looked desperate to see her as usual. He was all rumpled and gorgeous, though wearing precisely the kind of clothes Ashley did *not* want him to wear on Wednesday night—a ragged Death Cab T-shirt and jeans with a ripped pocket. She didn't want the world to think she was going out with a weepy emo boy, hello.

"Hey, Ashley," he said, looking around the room for somewhere to sit. Every possible surface, including the bed, was scattered with discarded clothes and accessories. She brushed a heap of bright H&M tops off a chaise, and he sat down, looking really awkward and weird.

Which was odd, since he had a bunch of sisters and should be used to all this girly stuff. Plus he spent a lot of time with A.A., although she was more like a guy, really, playing video games and talking about sports all the time. Ashley was more of a girly-girl, more of a lady. Which was why she was going to win *Preteen Queen* by a landslide.

"I'm so glad you're here," she told him, pushing one of the bureau drawers shut. "There's so much we have to do before Wednesday, and I—"

"I have to tell you something," he interrupted. He stared over at her, his face stricken. "It's about . . . something that happened last night."

"Last night?"

"Yeah, at the party," he said at last, looking away.

"What party?"

"The Seven party."

"You went?" Ashley accused, feeling betrayed. They had agreed that the party would be mega-lame. But maybe it was okay. Since she hadn't been at the party, what he was going to say wasn't about her at all. And if it wasn't about Ashley, it wasn't bound to be very interesting. She pushed some more clothes onto the floor so she could sit down for a minute on the window seat. All this trying-on was exhausting.

"Yeah, I went. And, anyway"—Tri bit his lip—"I kissed somebody. That's what I've come to tell you. I kissed someone else, and I think you and I should break up."

What? Tri kissed someone? Not Ashley, his publicly acknowledged, as-seen-on-TV girlfriend? The one he'd *never even kissed*? And now he wanted to *break up with her*? Three days before the *Preteen Queen* results party??

Ashley couldn't believe her ears. This was worse than the ending of *Titanic*, when Leonardo DiCaprio died. No hottie should freeze to death!

"I'm really sorry," Tri was saying. "I just don't think it's fair to you to keep going out when I like someone else."

He liked someone else??

Whaaaat??

This was even worse. Ashley had thought Tri just kissed some random girl and felt guilty. Now it seemed like he actually did it on purpose . . . because he *liked* this girl.

"Who is she?" she demanded, kicking at the nearest pile of clothes. "I can't believe she tried to move in on *my boyfriend!*"

"It's not like that!" Tri leaped to his feet and walked toward her—keeping just beyond kicking distance, she noticed. "She didn't even want to play Seven with me, but I said she had to! I nicked her phone and told her that rules were rules. I made her kiss me, okay? Because I wanted to. Because . . . I like her. I've always liked her."

Ashley felt like her head was about to explode. "You've always liked her?" she repeated. She felt a cold stab at her heart. It was her worst nightmare. She knew it before he confirmed it.

"It's A.A.," he said. "And don't be mad at her, okay? Like I said, she didn't want to kiss me. She's never liked me in that way, and she still doesn't. She has no idea that I'm here today breaking up with you or anything."

"Then why are you doing it?" said Ashley in a baby voice, tears of self-pity drizzling down her face. Tri liked A.A. He *preferred* her to Ashley. Why? Why? Why?

"Did you ever even like me at all?" Ashley wailed. "Just a little bit? I mean, we have a lot of fun together, right?"

"I *did* like you." Tri turned red. "At first. But I think I just felt really guilty about almost killing you. I was the one who brought you the cupcake. And you looked so vulnerable and helpless and . . . I dunno. I think going out with you was a mistake. I was just mad that A.A. thought some other guy was laxjock. I just wanted to make her jealous. But I didn't want to . . . I never wanted to hurt you."

Ashley sniffed, trying to look vulnerable and helpless again. She raised her doe eyes to him, hoping it would change his mind.

"But we're not meant to be," Tri said strongly. "I can't go out with you when I really like someone else. It's just not right. It would be a big lie."

"It's only a little lie," Ashley murmured, but Tri shook his head.

"If I'm going to have any chance with A.A., I have to break up with you. She'll never look at me if she thinks I'm her best friend's boyfriend. You know that."

Ashley rubbed her damp eyes with the back of her hand. She needed a plan, and she needed one quick, if this week wasn't going to be ruined.

"So you haven't told her you're breaking up with me," she said, her voice plaintive.

"Like I told you, no."

"You haven't told anyone?"

"No one. Honestly."

"Well." Ashley sighed, releasing the fluffy cushion she'd had in a death grip for the last five minutes. "Maybe you'd consider waiting a few days. For my sake."

Tri looked puzzled.

"What do you mean, waiting?"

"I mean waiting until after the party on Wednesday night. Just be my date one last time, and then we can break everything off. No tears, no recriminations. You'll be free to ask A.A. out, and I won't try and stop you."

"I don't know." Tri hesitated, jamming his hands in his pockets. "Why wait?"

"Because it's the most important night of my life, okay?" Ashley started crying again, thinking of the humiliation of turning up at the party without her supposedly in-love-with-her boyfriend. "And I don't want everyone asking mean questions. It's the least you can do for me, considering what you did to me last night."

Tri hung his head. He gave a long sigh.

"All right," he said. "I'll take you to the party, and then it's all over."

"And you won't say anything to A.A. until then?"

"No."

"Or anyone else?"

"No."

"Promise?"

"I promise," said Tri, looking totally miserable, and Ashley knew that he would keep his word.

208

28

JANE AUSTEN'S GOT NOTHING ON ASHLEY SPENCER

THE *PRETEEN QUEEN* RESULTS PARTY WAS HELD AT a hot new club downtown. A.A. drifted around the room, wishing the lights from the cameras weren't quite so bright: Her makeup felt like it was melting off her face. A giant screen hung on one wall, and there were TV monitors in every corner and above all the food stations. Each was tuned to a different *Preteen Queen* party in a different city.

The live broadcast on Sugar was about to run on the big screen, with Vanessa Minillo presenting from Los Angeles. Jasper, the British producer, had motioned A.A. over as soon as she arrived and told her that the San Francisco results would be announced last.

"We're having some last-minute technical difficulties,

unfortunately," he said, frowning at the Blackberry in his hand. "Nothing for you to worry about. Tiffany will give you the signal when we're ready for you girls, and then you should make your way to the marked spot in the middle of the room."

A.A. nodded, though she was only half listening. There were too many other things to worry about than the stupid vote tally. The sooner this show was over and done with, and she could get back to her normal/abnormal life, the sooner she might be able to get a clear head. Everything was so foggy right now. And by right now she meant SSN—Since Saturday Night. Why did Tri have to pick her phone out of the bowl? Why did he have to insist on kissing her? And why did she have to like it so much?

The room was already crowded with Miss Gamble's girls, almost the whole upper form and a bunch from the younger grades as well, all dressed to the nines, and a number of boys from Gregory Hall and Saint Aloysius. The photographer from the school newspaper was there, taking pictures for Miss Gamble's gossip column, "Page Seven." Lauren had arrived with a cute date. A.A. knew it—Lauren hadn't been lying. She wondered where Lauren's other guy was that evening. And Lili had swept in looking superchic, her hair in a perfect chignon, wearing a darling little navy dress—navy was apparently the new black.

A.A. half wished she'd gone to more trouble with her own outfit. Her mother had arranged for the professional makeup artist to come over to their penthouse suite after school, and then insisted that A.A. wear a lacy chiffon dress Jeanine had brought back from Argentina. A.A. had just done what she was told without arguing—and without caring. So what if she forgot to wear earrings, or if her lizard-skin bag didn't really go with her silver Choos? What did any of it matter?

All that mattered was that Tri hadn't called her. She'd thought for sure that things would change after they'd kissed in the closet. That night, when they'd finally had to stop kissing because another couple was banging on the door, the two of them hadn't even felt embarrassed about what had happened. Tri looked really happy. He couldn't stop grinning, and neither could A.A.

"I'll call you," he'd promised, and she'd nodded, still on cloud nine, her head spinning from that illicit kiss.

But there had been no calls. Nothing. Not a word. Not an e-mail. Not an IM.

A.A. was out of her mind, especially on Monday at school when Ashley mentioned in passing that Tri had been really sweet the day before, coming over to help her choose her outfit for the party. But there wasn't a chance to ask her any probing questions: Ashley was out of school with a "cold" all

Tuesday and Wednesday, although A.A. suspected it was just an excuse so that Ashley could avail herself of dozens of beauty treatments before the results taping.

Had she been wrong? A.A. had believed Tri was as much into the kiss as she'd been. She thought that he liked her as much as she liked him.

But if he felt that way, why hadn't he gotten in touch? Wouldn't he maybe think about breaking up with Ashley? Going over to her house to help her pick an outfit for the party didn't sound like someone who was planning to dump her. A.A. just didn't get it.

Meanwhile, Hunter was still totally into her, probably because he didn't know she'd had a tongue-fest in the closet with another guy. At the Seven party, he'd tracked her down after his poker game. The stupid boy had picked the wrong phone out of the bowl—one that was studded with rubies. They both felt the same, he explained, when you had a blind-fold on, but he swore he wouldn't kiss Miss Ruby Studs. A.A. had her own phone safely back in her bag at that point, and she told Hunter she was going home.

By Tuesday afternoon, when Tri still hadn't called and after the hundredth text message from Hunter, she finally relented and said Hunter could come to the *Preteen Queen* party.

It looked like it was a strictly one-kiss thing with Tri.

She felt totally dissed. There was no hope for anything else to develop.

Actually, if A.A. was being totally honest, she'd still had a glimmer of hope when she arrived at the party. But that was dashed the second she saw Ashley and Tri together, holding hands like they were Brad and Angelina. There was nothing she could do but sample some of the sushi and pomegranate iced tea, admire the tiara-shaped cake standing on a table near the center of the room, and wait for Hunter to arrive.

Ashley tracked her down in front of the buffet and beckoned her over to the window. The results from the Miami group were being announced on the big screen, and the screaming from that party was deafening.

"What do you think of my dress?" she gushed, doing a slow spin so A.A. could see the back. "It's Zac Posen."

"It's fabulous," A.A. said flatly, wishing that the party was over already. Ashley gripped A.A.'s arm and pulled her close.

"Don't say anything to anyone," Ashley confided, "not even Lili or Lauren, but . . . "

"But what?"

"I've decided to break up with Tri."

"Really?" A.A. was surprised and—she had to admit—not unhappy to hear this. Ever since the kiss, she'd felt a hurricane of different emotions. She couldn't stop thinking about him. One minute she was ecstatic, but the next she felt depressed because he still hadn't called.

Then she felt guilty about kissing her best friend's boyfriend, and strangely a little guilty about kissing someone who wasn't Hunter. She'd been desperate for Tri to call her, but she was also determined not to chase after him. But now Ashley was announcing that things with Tri and her were over.

"I've been meaning to do it for ages," Ashley explained. "That's why I didn't come to the party on Saturday. I told him that we should take a break, maybe, and start seeing other people. Not be so serious. But then he came over to my place on Sunday and was nearly in tears. I mean, it was *embarrassing*."

"Why? Did he cry or something?" A.A. scoffed. She couldn't see Tri doing anything that silly.

"Almost." Ashley reached for A.A.'s drink and took a long sip. "He said he couldn't stand it. He said he realized on Saturday night that no other girl was my equal, blah blah blah. He went on and on about how beautiful I was. I felt so bad for him. I think he might be in love with me. Can you believe it?"

A.A. shrugged.

"And he wanted to kiss me, so I agreed," Ashley continued. "I know, I know. I should have said no. But he's a pretty amazing kisser, and I couldn't resist. Sorry—is this TMI?"

"Whatever." A.A. felt sick. When Ashley handed her back the pomegranate tea, she set the cup on the windowsill.

"He told me that it was the best kiss of his life," Ashley stage-whispered. "So what was I supposed to do? I couldn't break up with him. I decided to wait until after this party."

"Good call," said A.A., when she realized that Ashley was waiting for a response. Everything she was wearing felt heavy, like it was a suit of armor rather than a chiffon dress.

"He was so freaked out at the idea of me coming to the party without him," Ashley said. "It would have been mean. And I do like Tri, I really do. Just not in that way. He's just a teddy bear. You understand, right?"

"Totally."

"I don't want to break his heart. He actually said that I was the most beautiful and interesting girl he'd ever met. Isn't that sweet? Maybe a little creepy, though. I'm going to end it tonight after the party, before he gets even more obsessed."

A.A. couldn't bring herself to speak. What a slimebag Tri was! First he kissed her like he meant it, then he ran back to Ashley, swearing undying love. Ashley had to be telling the truth. What else would explain the way Tri had avoided and/or ignored A.A. ever since Saturday night? He hadn't even *tried* to break up with Ashley. Here he was at the party, holding her hand and looking as devoted as ever. She wanted to slap him. He wouldn't even look in her direction!

"That guy's waving at you," Ashley told her, pointing over A.A.'s shoulder. "Is that Hunter? He's dishy."

A.A. spun around and saw Hunter walking toward her. He looked really hot in his Lacoste polo shirt and crisp pressed khakis, his red hair slicked down, his eyes sparkling. Sparkling at *her*. Here was a guy who really liked her. A guy who ran around trying to get her attention, sending her messages, asking her out. The show was on a commercial break, so music was blasting out of the speakers, and a DJ was shouting at everyone to dance.

"Wanna dance, Miss Preteen Queen?" Hunter shouted over the racket, and A.A. smiled at him, taking the hand he offered. Forget Tri and that stupid kiss. Maybe she'd kiss Hunter tonight, at the end of the party—and not in a closet, either. Ashley wasn't the only one who could have a boyfriend.

29

IS THIS THE END OF AN ERA?
OR JUST THE END OF THE ASHLEYS?

T HAD BEEN A LONG TIME SINCE THE COED mixer at Miss Gamble's, where Lauren was still a social pariah and saved the day only by—literally—saving Ashley's life. When she thought how terrified she'd been about walking into that party, how she'd come up with the ploy of dragging Billy Reddy along to give her some credibility, Lauren wasn't sure if she should laugh or cry. How things had changed!

Now she was one of the main attractions at the *Preteen Queen* results party. The photographer from the *Gambler*, the school newspaper, hustled her into a photo with the three Ashleys, all of them pouting and posing like the StripHall Queens—their favorite pop group. Ashley shoved her way into the middle, of course, practically elbowing Lili out of the way.

Guinevere Parker, who had managed to bag the job of social reporter, cornered Lauren to ask "who" she was wearing, so they could print every vital fashion detail.

"Is it true that you were the one approached by the TV show?" Guinevere asked, scribbling furiously in her flip-top notebook. The Ashleys were right: She did have a bobble-head. "Without you, none of this would have happened?"

"Well, I don't know about that." Lauren shrugged. She wanted to tell Guinevere that her friend Dex was right, you shouldn't care too much about what people thought, although it was a lot easier not to care when you knew everyone liked you. Or feared you. Or wanted to be you, somehow. That's why Ashley got away with being so mean, Lauren decided. Nobody would be snubbing *her* anytime soon. "It's true that the producers approached me, but the show was about all of us. And it's not really that big a deal. Really."

Though it was clearly a big-time biggie for Ashley herself, Lauren noticed. Ashley kept glancing up at the giant TV monitor, watching Vanessa read the results from different cities, even though everyone else was preoccupied with eating and dancing and waving at one another.

Lauren had decided to make the evening less stressful than Saturday's party by ensuring that only one of her guys was on the premises. After much careful thought—i.e., an hour-long phone call with Lili on Sunday—Lauren had invited Christian to come along to the results party.

Meanwhile, Alex was going to come over to her house later to hang out, eat dinner, and watch a tape of the show.

Her mother was so excited about A Real Boyfriend coming over to the house, she'd wanted to go completely over the top with all the arrangements: order an In-N-Out Burger mobile unit to set up in their front yard, get a new popcorn machine, and install an even bigger screen in the already gigantic screening room. All week her mother had driven their builders and decorator crazy with the new plans.

Thankfully, Lauren had succeeded in persuading her mother to forget about the renovation: They were only watching a DVD of a reality show, not the latest revised edition of *Star Wars*. Trudy had been madly disappointed that she wouldn't be allowed to do anything except greet the boy, and Lauren understood, kind of. For so long they had nothing. Now they had everything, and her mother wanted to make up for lost time. Trudy wanted Lauren to have the perfect teenage life, even if she wasn't quite a teenager yet.

"Lauren!" Christian bounded over, his shirt endearingly untucked as usual. He was clutching something in one hand— a Tiffany's box! "I was going to get you a corsage, but my mom told me you'd rather have something like this."

He handed her the box and Lauren beamed at him, carefully

untying the white ribbon. Guinevere stood peering over Christian's shoulder, noting down every detail. Lauren opened the box and pulled out a platinum charm in the shape of a crown. It was elegant and beautiful. Her first-ever present from a boy!

"It attaches to your phone," Christian explained, shifting from foot to foot. He was so sweet and diffident. Lauren felt bad that he wasn't the one coming over to her house tonight. This torn-between-two-lovers deal wasn't as exciting as it sounded. Just complicated and guilt-inducing.

"It's amazing," she told him. "I love it. But you know, I'm probably not going to win or anything."

"That doesn't matter," he said, clearly relieved that she liked the gift. "You're still . . . you know."

They both blushed, and Guinevere leaned in even farther. She was making a sketch of the charm in her notebook.

"What's the diameter of this, would you say?" she asked a bemused Christian, but before he could answer, Ashley pushed her way between them.

"What's that? A little charm? Cute!" Ashley fluttered her fingers at the charm like it was a baby bird. "Lauren, I need to talk to you. Someone just said that there were *big* changes today on AshleyRank."

"I didn't look at it today," Lauren said, a little annoyed that Ashley wanted to talk about this now. Couldn't she see that Lauren had a date? What did she care about the stupid blog right now?

"I heard that there are seismic changes in the top rankings," Guinevere chipped in, elbowing Christian out of the way so she could get closer to Ashley. Poor Christian! Lauren shot him an I'm-sorry-see-you-later smile and turned back to Ashley, who was glaring at Guinevere. Lauren hadn't seen Ashley this annoyed since someone dropped a piece of spelt bread on one of her Louboutin Mary Janes in the school refectory.

"What do you mean, exactly?" Ashley demanded.

"Well," Guinevere began, her voice trembling. She wasn't used to being addressed directly by Ashley Spencer, Lauren thought. It was all too much for her. "Lauren's moved from number ten to number three. It's her highest ranking ever."

"Really?" Lauren couldn't believe it. This had to be the work of Christian and Alex—both of them told her at the party on Saturday night that they'd checked out AshleyRank. If they'd both given her nines or even tens in each category, then this new ranking would make sense.

"What!" Ashley shrieked.

Lauren realized why she was freaking out: If Lauren was number three, it meant that one of the Ashleys had dropped out of the top three. They no longer ruled the school! Lauren had infiltrated their clique and nudged one of them out of the way! Forget *Preteen Queen*—this was the real barometer of cool. And the bottom line was, Lauren's plan had worked! She was one of them! But now that she'd gotten what she wanted, did she still want to destroy them? Lauren wasn't so sure anymore.

"You mean to tell me that Lili is number four now?" Ashley demanded.

"Oh, no," Guinevere said, shaking her head. "Lauren moving up isn't the only change. Lili's moved up as well. She's number one."

Ashley was ivory pale at the best of times, but now she was white as a sheet. She rocked backward a little, like she was unsteady on her feet. It looked as though she was about to faint, and this time no trace of nuts was involved. Lauren grabbed Ashley's arm to steady her. The *Preteen Queen* results were about to be announced—Ashley couldn't collapse!

"So what you're telling me," Ashley said, fixing Guinevere with a death stare, "is that I am now *number two* in the rankings?"

"Er . . . not exactly." Guinevere took a step back, glancing over at the exit sign as though she were planning a quick escape. "A.A. is number two. You're number four."

For the first time ever in living memory—or at least Lauren's memory—Ashley Spencer was speechless.

30

THE VIEW FROM THE TOP

LILI WAS ECSTATIC! EVERYONE AT THE *PRETEEN Queen* party was buzzing with the news that she had soared to the top of AshleyRank. Poor Lauren was trying to persuade Ashley that she had nothing to do with it—that she wasn't behind the blog in any way, and that she was as surprised as anyone at the shift in rankings.

"Can you believe it?" A.A. asked Lili as they made their way to the marked spot in the center of the room. The San Francisco results were about to be announced, and a frazzled production assistant with a headset and clipboard was trying to round up the Ashleys. Ashley was still holed up in the bathroom, fanning herself with Guinevere Parker's notebook and screaming at Lauren.

"I don't know," said Lili, practically skipping to her spot. What she meant was, she didn't care. She was number one at last! How it happened wasn't really clear. Ever since the *Preteen Queen* broadcast, Lili had felt like everything was slipping away.

Max rejected her and then snubbed her at French class. He hadn't even bothered to turn up this week, probably because his new girlfriend was taking up all his free time. Everyone at school was still smirking about the hidden camera footage. And at the party on Saturday night she'd felt like a child sent to sit on the naughty stool in the corner. Lili felt really great in the dress she'd borrowed from A.A., but after Max showed up, all her positive feelings disintegrated into misery and shame. She'd gone home early, reconciling herself to a lonely single life and perpetual social shame.

But now things were looking up at last!

"We need the other two!" Matt snapped at the production assistant. "We have enough problems tonight without the talent going missing."

"He's in a bad mood," A.A. observed to the PA, who gave a despondent shrug.

"I don't even know if this is going to happen," the PA muttered, hurrying off in search of Ashley and Lauren.

"Did you hear that?" A.A. asked Lili. "What do you think she meant?"

"I don't know," Lili said. Her head was still reeling from hearing that she was number one. Was it even true? How was this possible? It was everything she'd dreamed of since she'd first heard about AshleyRank.

"Okay—now stay here!" Another production assistant was dragging Ashley and Lauren toward them.

Ashley, who was puffy-eyed, was still harassing Lauren. "I know it was you. Admit it, you're the one behind AshleyRank. Especially since you're the only one who's benefited from it."

"You've got to believe me, I had absolutely nothing to do with it!" Lauren protested.

"But your dad runs that tech company!"

"We own a video-sharing website. What does that have to do with anything? Lots of people in San Francisco own tech companies. Duh. It doesn't mean we have some inside connection to anyone's blog."

Ashley looked stumped for a moment. "But your driver—Dex—he's like some programming genius. . . ."

Lauren rolled her eyes. "I can assure you, Dex has better things to do than follow us around. Get serious, Ashley."

"C'mon, Ash, pull yourself together," Lili urged, giving her the sweetest smile. Now wasn't the time to rub in her triumph. She would wait . . . let's see, maybe five minutes?

Lauren was smoothing down her hair, still looking kind of shell-shocked after Ashley's attack. If she was really the one behind AshleyRank, then she was pretty brave—and/or foolish—

kicking Ashley out of the top three. If she *wasn't* the one writing the blog, then it was pretty unfair of Ashley to go postal on her. But someone had to be the fall guy, and Lili was a little glad that Ashley wasn't venting her rage on her

A TV camera was pointed in their direction, its red light on, and Lili made sure she was smiling straight into the lens. Finally deciding to drop the subject, Ashley wriggled her way into the center as usual and pasted the fakest smile ever on her face. Lili couldn't help admiring her. Even in a moment of disaster, Ashley could rise above her distress, and look as serenely perfect as ever.

"Everyone quiet!" shouted someone—it sounded like Matt—and the room was hushed. "We're on in ten seconds."

Lili looked up at the big screen for a few seconds to see what was happening. Vanessa had been handed a piece of paper and she was staring at it, not saying anything.

A.A. grabbed Lili's hand and squeezed it. "I feel like a dork," she whispered.

"Shut up and smile!" Lili whispered back, gritting her teeth.

"Why don't *you* shut up?" hissed Ashley, probably thinking that Lili was talking to her.

"Don't forget we're being filmed!" Lauren murmured out of the side of her mouth.

"I'm sorry." Vanessa Minillo's voice boomed through the

room. "I've just been told we can't announce the San Francisco results tonight. The servers are still down. Sorry about this! We're going to go back to the victory party in Dallas, where I hear a food fight has broken out among the unsuccessful contestants. Over to Dallas!"

The Ashleys stood staring at each other, stupefied, as the noise level in the room reached an all-time high. Lili couldn't believe it, and clearly nobody else could either.

"You mean, that's it?" A.A. asked. "Can we go home now?"

"I guess," said Lauren uncertainly. "At least, do we still have to stand here?"

"This is a total travesty," raged Ashley, hands on hips, her eyes flashing fire. "They'll be hearing from my dad's lawyer about this."

"Maybe they could sue AshleyRank as well." Lili couldn't resist the snarky comment.

"What is that supposed to mean?" demanded Ashley.

"You know—for crimes against Ashley?"

"Oh God," A.A. groaned. "I'm going to get some more food. Hunter's waiting for me with a plate of shrimp tempura and it's probably freezing by now."

"And I'm going to find Christian," said Lauren quickly, scanning the room. "And Guinevere, because she's still got the charm he gave me."

"Ladies, ladies, we are so sorry." Tiffany, the third producer, rushed toward them. "This is a disaster! There's a blackout at headquarters and the generator won't kick in."

"Whatever!" said Ashley, holding up a hand. She gave a loud sniffle. "I need to look for my boyfriend! Where is he?"

God, Ashley is so jealous, Lili thought. She couldn't stand the other girls having boys hanging around, and she couldn't stand Lili being number one on AshleyRank. Lili saw Ashley approach Tri with her sob story, but Tri pushed her away with an angry look on his face. Tri was staring at Hunter and A.A., who were slow-dancing to a song.

Then Lili noticed someone else.

Someone looking straight at her. Someone blond, dark-eyed, and unbearably cute.

Max.

All Lili's resolve to never look at, speak to, or approach Max again flew out the window. When he caught her eye, he didn't turn away this time. Instead he smiled, and she smiled back and began to walk toward him. Why was he here? What did he want?

"Lili," he said, hurrying up to meet her halfway. "I'm sorry to crash your event like this, but I had to talk to you."

Lili couldn't trust herself to reply. She looked up at Max's handsome, frowning face and felt her heart performing a triple toe loop.

"I wanted to tell you I was sorry," he continued. "About— you know. Walking out on you at the party the way I did. Not

228

calling you. Not speaking to you at all at Madame's. I've been a real idiot. And then I saw you at the party last weekend, but you disappeared before I had to chance to say anything."

"Well, you were with another girl," Lili reminded him.

"She's just a friend."

"Really?"

"Really," Max assured her. "Anyway . . . I'm sorry. I just thought—I don't know, that we were moving too fast. I mean . . . I like you and . . . What I'm trying to say is, I guess I've never had a girlfriend before and . . ."

Lili wished the cameras were here now so she could relive this moment until eternity. Max admitted he liked her! And he'd mentioned the sweetest word a girl could hear. "Girlfriend." Did this mean . . . ?

"Anyway, do you want to go grab some food or something? Get out of here? Those screaming girls are kind of freaking me out," he said, looking over his shoulder at a group of giggling sixth graders who were eavesdropping on their conversation.

He looked so anxious and nervous and cute, and Lili understood that his fate was in her hands. She could choose to be with Max, or she could choose not to be with him. It was her prerogative, like the Britney Spears cover of that old Bobby Brown song.

"Sure," Lili said, taking the hand he was offering. His

hands were cold from the air-conditioning, and Lili felt a pang at how vulnerable he really was. He wasn't some unfeeling jerk. He was just human. They were going to go grab a bite to eat, and then . . . maybe they would kiss again. Lili hoped there would be a lot of kissing in her future.

Max grinned his shy, sleepy grin, and at that moment, Lili wasn't jealous of anyone. She was just glad to be herself.

EPILOGUES

Dear Diary,

I'm sorry I haven't written much lately. My life's kind of crazy these days, ever since I acquired not one but two boyfriends. How did this happen?

I still can't decide which one I like the best. So for now I've decided to avoid any sort of social situation where the two guys could end up bumping into each other. I'm a strictly one-on-one girl, for now anyway. If only my mother can keep their names straight, I might get away with it.

Speaking of results shows, we got the call a week later from the Preteen Queen producers. They finally got the server back online, and the machine spit out the winner.

It was Ashley Spencer, of course.

Her triumph was short-lived, I'm glad to report. The network decided not to pick up the series, so there's no second round in a New York City penthouse apartment. Preteen Queen is dead. Long live whatever else Ashley decides to win in the future.

She's pretending she doesn't care, but I can tell she's mad

as hell. At least she's got something else to fume about aside from Ashley Rank. Which, by the way, has nothing to do with me. A group of sixth graders finally came forward to claim credit. Apparently they've been obsessed with the Ashleys since prekindergarten. Anyway, they're tired of writing about us and have started their own site: The Madisons. The kids are all right!

Till next time,
Lauren Page

MEMO: FILE: DIARY: ALIOTO, ASHLEY

IT'S OFFICIAL. I HAVE A B-FRIEND. HUNTER IS
COOL & I CAN TRUST HIM. UNLIKE TRI, MY EX
BFF. ASHLEY DUMPED HIM BUT IT'S 2 LATE.
I'VE MOVED ON, YO!

SO WHY AM I STILL NOT HAPPY?
A.A. ☹

Hello? Ready? Last time my voice came out all muffled, like I had a cold. Stupid gadget. Maria? I hope you can understand my voice this time. I'll speak r-e-a-l-l-l-l-y slowly.

Anyway, I won the *Preteen Queen* contest. Hello! Who else was going to win? Loser Lauren? Lili-I-Got-Dumped-on-National-TV? A.A. the tramp? I don't think so. I should have won by a landslide, but instead the margin of victory was . . . oh, who cares. I stopped listening when I heard my name. I don't even know who came in second.

The show was canceled, but whatever! I'm too busy to go to New York right now, anyway. Ever since I found out that stupid AshleyRank was run by a group of nerdy sixth graders obsessed with the Ashleys, I've been working with my father's lawyer to have it closed down. They're lucky I decided against suing for defamation. I mean, a two for my smile? As if!

Tri and I have split. Good riddance, that's what I say. He's too short and too immature. I'm only going to consider *taller* boys from now on. Everyone else seems to have a new boyfriend, so snagging one should be supereasy for me.

Maybe even snagging one of theirs . . .

Watch this space!

I haven't been on top of my journal work this week. Having a boyfriend is a lot of work! I hardly have time to see Max, and hope that those Reed Prep hoochies don't get their claws in him again.

Anyway, ever since I took over the number one spot on AshleyRank, things have changed. Strangely enough, Lauren seems more of an Ashley these days than Ashley. She has two boyfriends. I have a boyfriend. A.A. has a boyfriend. Ashley has no one! She says she broke up with Tri, but between you, me, and the grapevine, I don't think he was all that upset about it. I have Guinevere Parker investigating. (BTW, I don't believe the rumor that it was the sixth graders behind AshleyRank—my money's on Miss Gamble's own tabloid journalist.)

Ashley may have closed down the blog, but nobody at Miss Gamble's is going to forget she scored a two for smile. She's letting the Ashleys down! Doesn't she know we have a reputation to maintain?

Maybe it's time for us to reconsider our position. Should Ashley get kicked out of the Ashleys?

Yours in serious consideration,
Lili

HEAR YE, HEAR YE. WE NOW CROWN A NEW QUEEN of the Rank. For the first time since the inauguration of our little social experiment, we've got a new winner of the seventh-grade sweepstakes!

#1 ASHLEY "LILI" LI

Because every lax king needs a queen.

Enjoy your reign, and don't forget the little people!

STYLE: 10

Could probably wear a sack and make it work.

SOCIAL PRESENCE: 10

Tamed the biggest player at Reed Prep.

(And we don't mean lacrosse!)

SMILE: 10

It's official: It's megawatt.

SMARTS: 9

What do you call a girl who claws her way

to the top but still comes out smelling like a rose?

Brilliant!

CUMULATIVE SCORE: 39   (Because no one's perfect!)

#2 ASHLEY "A.A." ALIOTO

There's nothing we like more than a girl in love.

STYLE: 10

Proves you don't have to match your shoes

to your handbag to look good!

SOCIAL PRESENCE: 10

Her new BF is gorge! We love redheads too!

SMILE: 8

Smiles as if her heart is breaking . . . why is that?

SMARTS: 10

Unlike other girls we won't mention, this one

doesn't kiss and tell. . . .

CUMULATIVE SCORE: 38

next >>

#3 LAUREN PAGE

The Cinderella story of the semester!

STYLE: 10

Is it her new wide-leg Rich & Skinny jeans or the way she walks in them, as if she owns the world, that we like so much?

SOCIAL PRESENCE: 10

No slouch in the boyfriend—or should we say boyfriends—department either.

SMILE: 10

Totally bubbly these days.

SMARTS: 6

It's foolish to toy with boys' affections— they're not the only ones who could get hurt!

CUMULATIVE SCORE: 36

#4 ASHLEY SPENCER

The former Queen Bee has lost her buzz. . . .

STYLE: 7

For once, we find her outfits a little too contrived.

SOCIAL PRESENCE: 8

Ouch! She's been recently dumped by her
boyfriend *and* the network.

SMILE: 4

Oh, pookie. Things can only get better.

SMARTS: 8

Don't count her out yet. She's bound to have
more tricks up her Paul & Joe sleeve.

CUMULATIVE SCORE: 27

ACKNOWLEDGMENTS

any thanks to Emily Meehan, Courtney Bongiolatti, Richard Abate, Josie Freedman, Paula Morris, Christina Green, Jennie Kim, and Arisa Chen.

Love to everyone in my family, especially Mike & Mattie.

Thanks to all my readers. You're all numero uno in my book! Kisses!

ABOUT THE AUTHOR

Melissa de la Cruz once received a "four" for Funny and has (almost) forgiven the friend who gave it to her. She has written many books for teens, including the bestselling series The Au Pairs, Angels on Sunset Boulevard, and Blue Bloods. She lives in Los Angeles with her husband and daughter.

Check out her website at www.melissa-delacruz.com and send her an e-mail at melissa@melissa-delacruz.com.

Get ready
for the newest
Private novel:

Real life. Real you.

Don't miss any of these terrific Aladdin Mix books.

1-4169-3503-7 (paperback)

1-4169-5068-0 (paperback)

0-689-86614-3 (hardcover)
0-689-86615-1 (paperback)

1-4169-0867-5 (hardcover)
1-4169-5484-8 (paperback)

1-4169-3598-3 (paperback)

0-689-83957-X (hardcover)
0-689-83958-8 (paperback)

1-4169-0861-7 (hardcover)
1-4169-4739-6 (paperback)

1-4169-3519-3 (paperback)

1-4169-4893-7 (paperback)

1-4169-0930-3 (hardcover)
1-4169-0931-1 (paperback)

"Nothing is more glam than a summer in the Hamptons." —*Teen Vogue*

"It's all too fabulous for words." —*Village Voice*

"Fans of the Gossip Girl series will love this novel." —*Teenreads.com*

the au pairs

"A guilty-pleasure beach read!" —*Seventeen*

A NOVEL BY

melissa de la cruz

"This is *Sex and the City* lite, where everyone is a little more fabulous, flirtatious, snobby, and deceitful than we are—and it's quite all right with us."—*Romantic Times Book Club*

"The ultimate summer."—*YM*

Published by
Simon & Schuster